He would only help if she agreed to go out with him, but the last thing she wanted was to date a Marine...

The looks on his three friends' faces told Dylan he might regret this. "Oookkaay," he said, drawing out the word. "What's up?"

"One of the men for the bachelor auction had to cancel at the last minute and we need you to fill in for him. Please!" Brenda pleaded.

His jaw fell open. "Excuse me?" He glanced from one hopeful expression to the other, shook his head, and started to chuckle. "No way. Absolutely not!" he declared emphatically.

"Oh come on, Dylan. It's for charity. It's for the hospital," Veronica begged, appealing to his compassionate side.

Noticing Tessa had been silent this entire time, he turned his attention to her. "What do you think, Ms. Matthews?"

His question caught her off guard. She blushed and fidgeted slightly in her chair. "I think it would be kind and generous of you to help out." She paused. "But the decision is yours."

Dylan studied her for a few seconds. "All right, but only on one condition." The three women leaned closer in anticipation of his demand. "I'll contribute a thousand dollars and Tessa has to use that money to bid on me for the dinner date."

Tessa blinked, inhaled sharply, and sat back in her chair as if she'd been forcefully pushed there. With all eyes focused on her, she scanned the faces at the table. "I—I—but—"

"If she doesn't agree, the deal's off."

He'd make the perfect husband—if he wasn't a Marine...

After her husband is killed in Iraq, Tessa Matthews makes a promise to herself—never date another man in the military. Especially a Marine. A flat tire and dead cell phone threaten to challenge that vow when Gunnery Sergeant Dylan Cooper comes to her rescue. But can she ever allow herself to love a Marine—again?

He loves her but being a Marine is all he knows...

Dylan has never wanted any other occupation than being in the military, but now he's in conflict. He knows Tessa cares for him, but she won't allow herself to trust him or let the relationship develop past friendship as long as he's a Marine. He's also keeping an important secret from her that could end their relationship.

When the truth comes out, Tessa is devastated. How can she trust him with her heart when he could be killed at any moment?

KUDOS for *To Love a Marine*

In *To Love a Marine* by Debbie Lee, Tessa Mathews is a recent widow who lost her Marine husband to the war in the Middle East. Afraid to love a military man again, she denies her attraction to the handsome Marine sergeant, Dylan Cooper, who stops to help her change a flat tire. He is determined to win her, despite her resistance. But when he finally does, she discovers a secret that could destroy their relationship. *To Love a Marine* is the second book from Lee. And while the first book was a good offering for a new author, Lee seems to come into her own on this second one. *To Love a Marine* is a touching and poignant story of loss, grief, and true *love. ~ Taylor Jones, Reviewer*

To love a Marine by Debbie Lee is a heart-breakingly touching story of an all too real situation that many young women find themselves in today. Tessa Mathews married the love of her life and when he was killed in Iraq where he was deployed as a Marine, she decided the pain was too great and she wouldn't fall for another military man. But she hadn't counted on the handsome, and persistent, marine sergeant Dylan Cooper, who is relentlessly wearing down her resistance with charm and compassion. When she falls, she falls hard. Then she discovers that he can't stay. Now her heart is breaking again. I thought the story was very well-written. Lee handled the difficult subject with sensitivity and compassion. I could really relate to Tessa as she struggled to keep her heart from being broken again, even though she knew she was doomed from the start. The story is warm, sweet, touching, and has an authentic ring of truth that was almost painful at times. *~ Regan Murphy, Reviewer*

ACKNOWLEDGEMENTS

First and foremost, I thank God for His love and guidance. If it wasn't for Him, this book wouldn't exist. My life would be meaningless without Him.

A very special thank you to two men who I feel extremely privileged to know and to call my friends: Richard Perez, USMC Gunnery Sergeant, Retired, and Milton Hawkins, Jr., USMC Gunnery Sergeant, Retired.

TO LOVE
A MARINE

DEBBIE LEE

A Black Opal Books Publication

GENRE: CONTEMPORARY ROMANCE/MEN IN UNIFORM

This is a work of fiction. Names, places, characters and incidents are either the product of the author's imagination or are used fictitiously, and any resemblance to any actual persons, living or dead, businesses, organizations, events or locales is entirely coincidental. All trademarks, service marks, registered trademarks, and registered service marks are the property of their respective owners and are used herein for identification purposes only. The publisher does not have any control over or assume any responsibility for author or third-party websites or their contents. Any military bases, building, or installations used or mentioned in this book are not intended to be realistic or factual representations of any actual military bases, building, or installations, but are only intended to be fictional representations.

DEDICATION

*A deep and heartfelt thanks to all the men and women
who have bravely and unselfishly served this country,
past and present. Including my precious daughter,
Katie LaRose, 7 years in the USMC.*

*A tremendous amount of gratitude is due the spouses left
behind to carry on and keep the family together.
Thank you for your dedication and sacrifices.
You do not get nearly enough of the recognition
and thanks you so richly deserve.*

God Bless you all!

CHAPTER 1

Rifle fire pierced the still morning air. With each shot, Tessa Matthews felt a deep stab of pain in the middle of her chest. Off to the left, seven stone-faced Marines in their dress blues stood waiting to complete the task that had been asked of them. Each movement was precise and tightly synchronized as they readied themselves for the next pull of the trigger. Their highly polished black shoes glistened in the sun against the emerald green carpet of grass. Behind them, rows of white marble headstones gave testament to the other brave men and women who had found their final resting place at Arlington National Cemetery.

Even though the temperature was nearing a pleasant eighty degrees, Tessa shivered as a chill rushed through her. One she felt penetrate deep into her bones. Sitting on the folding chair in her simple black dress, she stared through dark sunglasses at the flag covered casket in front of her. The last thing her husband, Ben, had said to her was that he'd be home in about a month, just in time for their wedding anniversary. It turned out he'd been right—but not like they had planned.

The third and final round of gunfire broke through Tessa's wandering thoughts, bringing her back to the painful reality surrounding her. A sea of black enveloped her, friends and family who'd come to pay their last respects. Her parents sat on one side and Ben's on the other. She could hear crying behind her. In some odd way, it gave her comfort to know that so many people cared about him. Yet, she also believed, that for them, the unfortunate incident would soon become only a sad, fading memory. For Tessa, it was just the beginning of a hollow and excruciatingly lonesome existence. Now she had to figure out how to go on without him. How to live each day and pretend things were going to be all right. But they weren't—not ever. There would always be this gaping hole in her heart that nothing could ever fill.

Four Marines approached Ben's casket, two on each side. Reverently and solemnly they lifted the American flag that had been draped over the top. With meticulous precision, two of the men folded it thirteen times, forming a tight triangle with the bright white stars facing up against the field of deep blue.

One of the men approached Tessa and presented it to her. Then without a word, he quickly turned and walked away. Closing her eyes, she hugged it against her chest for a moment before placing it on her lap.

After the Chaplin finished speaking, she felt every muscle in her body tense as she watched a young Marine lift a shiny brass bugle to his lips. At the sound of the first note, she knew she wouldn't be able to hold back the heartbreaking tears welling up within her any longer. Taps. The haunting melody ripped at her heart. She pressed a linen hankie to her nose until he lowered the horn.

It was over.

People came up to her and expressed their condolences. They commented on how strong and brave she'd been for being able to hold it together during the service. She didn't even have the energy to fake a smile, so she just nodded. Tessa had heard all the encouraging words she could stomach since news had gotten out that her husband had died. She'd been told that it would get easier with time, that she'd get over the heartache and find someone else. *How dare they trivialize Ben's death*!

She felt as if they were talking about him like the passing of the family goldfish. Something easily replaceable. Then they assumed her life would simply carry on. She knew they meant well, but it took all the strength she had not to scream.

Her love for him would last forever. No one could

ever take his place in her heart. Not in a month, not in a year.

Not ever.

Over the last couple of weeks, Tessa had felt as if she had been drowning in her unbearable grief and loss. She'd wept for the man she loved. For the children they'd never have. And for their future together that had been stolen.

There would be no happily-ever-after.

CHAPTER 2

Eleven months later:

Tessa had been shopping all morning for a baby shower gift for one friend, as well as a wedding present for another. At first, she welcomed the distraction, anything to get her out of the house. Some days it was just too difficult to be there, it was too lonely. Other times it seemed as if the memories that lay in the walls were trying to swallow her up. They would close in on her. She felt suffocated and trapped. But now she was tired and ready to go home. Driving down the freeway, she let her mind drift to the beautifully wrapped packages in the backseat: two new beginnings—neither of which she would experience.

One because of war, one because of choice.

There was no husband, so there would be no baby.

A sudden, unmistakable vibration shook the car, pulling her from the depressing thoughts running through her mind.

A flat tire.

Maneuvering her crippled vehicle slowly to the right, she parked on the shoulder of the road. Tessa released a heavy sigh of frustration, leaning her forehead against her knuckles as they gripped the steering wheel.

"I don't need this right now."

After a moment or two, she raised her head and checked the driver's side mirror for a break in the traffic. Opening her door, she stepped out to survey the damage. She had the basic knowledge of what went where in order to change a flat, but that didn't mean she was willing to give it try. She kicked at the deflated tire with the toe of her shoe. She wasn't quite sure why, but from what she had witnessed other people do and what she had seen on TV, it was what you were expected to do in this type of situation. She walked around to the passenger side door, leaned through the open window, and dug her cell phone out of the cavernous pit she called a purse.

"Great! The battery's dead," Tessa vented as she tossed the useless device back into the expensive leather black hole. Reaching across the passenger seat, she switched on the emergency flashers. "Since I can't call roadside assistance, I guess I have no other choice but to wait and hope someone will stop to help me," she muttered.

Dylan Cooper sped down the H-1, heading to his buddy's house to watch the game. It was one of the major highways on the island and was always busy, but especially so on the weekends. When he rounded a curve, the traffic slowed, probably due to an accident or road construction up ahead. Not what he needed. He was already running late. He was usually in a hurry, but now he took a moment to enjoy the beautiful surroundings of the city he was lucky enough to call home—Honolulu, Hawaii. His eyes drank in the vivid blues and aquas of the ocean as well as the vibrant shades of green in the lush grasses and trees. That was when he noticed a woman standing next to a vehicle on the side of the road a little ways ahead of him. When he drove closer, he saw the problem.

He shook his head. "A helpless female who probably doesn't know the difference between oil and wiper fluid," he groused.

Immediately after he spoke those words, the scowling face of his granddad popped into his mind. It reminded him that he'd been raised to be a gentleman. Dylan's heart warmed with love for the man who had been the primary male influence in his life after his father died when Dylan was only ten. His mom's father had always been there for him to help him, talk to him, and lecture him when he needed it. Even though his granddad had passed away six years ago, Dylan still felt his presence from time to time. He tried to live his life in a manner that would've made him proud.

Glancing at his watch, he realized the game had already started, and his friends were going to give him hell. Yet he steered his 4x4 in the woman's direction, lane by lane, and parked behind her car.

Tessa had waited for almost twenty minutes before someone finally pulled over. Thankful chivalry wasn't dead, she watched the man slide out from behind the driver's side door. His black T-shirt was molded to his muscular chest like a second skin, and his long legs were encased in a pair of well-worn jeans.

She offered him a grateful smile. "Thank you for stopping."

He nodded in response. "Can you pop the trunk please, ma'am? Do you know if you have a spare and a jack?"

"I have no idea. My husband—" Emotions suddenly caused her eyes to well up, and she quickly swiped at a single tear. She didn't want to cry in front of a stranger, but sometimes they broke free and took her by surprise. It had been that kind of day.

Oh, great, Dylan thought while he raised the trunk lid. Leaning inside, he located the jack then lifted up the carpet to retrieve the donut. He bounced it on the asphalt and was relieved it appeared to be in good shape.

Tessa studied his profile while he worked. His hair was black, cut short on the sides and a little longer on top, a typical Marine high-and-tight. He had a square jaw and a nose that was a tad crooked, as if maybe it had been broken once. *Probably in a fight*, she thought. His biceps strained against the black cotton material as he worked to loosen each lug nut. Even behind his dark sunglasses, she could see that he was ruggedly handsome. One-hundred-percent American male. In that very second, she realized her pulse had increased during her assessment of this Good Samaritan. It startled her and a pang of guilt jabbed at her heart. She shouldn't have this reaction. It hadn't been that long ago since Ben had died, and these feelings were absolutely inappropriate.

And definitely unwelcome.

It only took Dylan a few minutes to switch tires and toss the damaged one in the trunk along with the jack. He wiped his hands on a rag he retrieved from his truck. "That should get you to a repair shop, ma'am. Just don't wait too long."

"I appreciate you taking the time to help me."

"No problem," he said with a slight grin.

As he looked at her, a gentle breeze danced through a few strands of her honey-colored hair. She was pretty. The girl-next-door kind of pretty, but maybe kicked up a notch or two. A pleasant scent drifted up to his nose. It was hard to pinpoint exactly.

He smelled something fresh and flowery above the exhaust of the passing vehicles. As his appraisal contin-ued, he discovered this woman definitely had the kind of body that could get a man's attention. He would have turned on the charm and asked her out, but she mentioned a husband. He didn't go after what belonged to somebody else.

Right before he left, he caught sight of the Marine Corp decal in the back window and a "Marine Wife" bumper sticker. His initial annoyance eased some, knowing he'd helped a fellow leatherneck's wife.

"What company is your husband with?" he said, motioning with his head."

Tessa lowered her head and wrapped one arm across her ribs. With the other hand, she reached for the gold chain that always lay draped around her neck. Glancing up into his face, she answered so softly that he almost didn't hear her, especially above the hum of the traffic in the background.

"He—he was killed in action a few months ago in Iraq."

Dylan's heart sank. "I'm very sorry to hear that, ma'am. I've lost some good friends over there."

It was her turn to nod. Pain lodged in her throat, making it impossible to verbally respond.

"I better get going. Don't drive too fast on that spare," he said, pointing at the small rubber donut. Their eyes held and he hesitated a moment. Waiting. As if somehow he sensed their conversation wasn't quite finished.

Finally, Tessa broke the silence. "I'll be careful and

thanks again, Mr…um…" She hesitated and her voice trailed off.

He extended his hand. "Dylan Cooper."

"Tessa. Tessa Matthews," she said, placing her hand in his.

It was large and calloused, enveloping hers like a baseball in a catcher's mitt. A tingle shot down her spine. Another sensation she forced herself to ignore. It was too soon for her to be attracted to another man.

Besides, he was a Marine—and that made him off limits.

They said their goodbyes, and she watched him climb back up into his big, black truck. He lifted a hand to wave before merging into traffic and driving off down the road.

Feeling exhausted, Tessa headed for home to take a long, hot bath and have a glass of wine. The tire would have to wait until tomorrow.

ﾟﾟﾟ

As soon as Dylan arrived at Eddie's house, the complaints started.

Eddie pointed at his watch. "Do you know what time it is, dude?"

"You're late. The game's half over," Joe chimed in, stating the obvious.

"Where've you been?" Eddie pressed.

"I stopped to help a woman with a flat tire," Dylan said and related the story of what happened.

Eddie walked over to the living room window, pushed the curtain aside, and peered out.

"What are you doing?" Eddie's wife, Karen, asked stepping into the room.

"I'm looking to see where Sir Galahad left his white horse and suit of armor."

"Funny," Dylan grunted. "Very funny."

After seeing the confusion on his wife's face, Eddie explained what was going on.

"That was so sweet of you," she said, smiling at their guest. "It's good to know that there are still some *real* gentlemen left in this world," she added, shooting an accusing glare in the direction of her husband.

"What?" Eddie asked innocently and shrugged. Karen's facial expression and body language silently challenged him. "Hey, when you had car trouble last month I was there for you, wasn't I?" he said, defending himself as he walked back toward the couch.

She arched her eyebrows, folded her arms across her chest, and cocked one hip to the side. "You called triple A." Her stance was the universal sign wives used to let husbands know they had just said something really stupid.

"Exactly. See, I didn't leave you stranded," Eddie agreed proudly, positive he had won this debate. He glanced over at his friends for back up.

They just smiled at him with *you're-so-busted* expressions.

Karen shook her head then turned around and marched out of the room, mumbling something under her breath the men couldn't hear.

"Hey, Dylan, you wanna beer?" Eddie offered.

"Sure, just let me wash up first."

CHAPTER 3

At work Friday morning, Tessa and Michelle stood in the staff lounge, one making coffee, the other toasting a bagel. The window-less room was bland and boring. The only decoration was an old, faded painting left over from someone's garage sale that hung a little askew on one of the stark white walls. There were two large bulletin boards plastered with all the standard, mandatory posters from the HR department. Any free space was filled with flyers of miscellaneous items for sale by employees and a few random restaurant menus. Chipped, gray Formica covered the four tables. Staff quickly learned to be careful not to scratch an elbow or snag a favorite shirt. Mismatched plastic chairs with metal legs completed the borderline institutional look of the room. The executives at the insurance company where the women worked promised this area was next in line for a "face-lift" on their list of upgrades throughout the building. Everyone hoped it would happen sooner rather than later. Their offices recently moved because the business was expanding and they required additional personnel.

Tessa heard a rhythmic clicking on the black and white tile floor in the hallway. The unmistakable sound announced her friend's arrival before she actually came into view. Turning toward the door, the two women leaned back against the counter in front of the microwave, patiently anticipating what the third member of their trio would be wearing today. It was a daily ritual they found amusing.

With her morning Starbucks in her right hand and the straps of a designer purse nestled in the crook of her left elbow, Brenda strutted into the room. Her brown hair flowed down her back, glistening like melted milk chocolate. She was a beautiful woman inside. Outside she had that indefinable "it" factor, always turning heads every time she entered a room. Today, she was "decked out" in a colorful spring dress that showed off her Sports Illustrated swimsuit-model figure, and bright fuchsia, five-inch heels. She was one-hundred percent girly-girl. She always chose her necklace, earrings, and bracelets with great care, accessorizing her outfit down to the last detail. The color of her nail polish even matched her shoes.

Those so-called "fashion experts" in New York and L.A. had nothing on her.

Brenda smiled. "Good morning, ladies."

Both women did a quick scan of their friend's outfit.

"*Another* new pair of shoes?" It mystified and intrigued Tessa how some women seemed to be obsessed with torturing their feet for the sake of style.

"I saw them online and simply couldn't resist." Beaming down at her most recent acquisition, Brenda extended her leg forward and pivoted the toe of her right foot on the tile to show them off. "Aren't they adorable?"

Michelle stirred another packet of artificial sweetener into her coffee. The metal spoon clinked against the sides of a red, ceramic mug. Bold, white lettering clearly broadcast the self-proclaimed, and unapologetic, opinion she had of herself. *Babe-a-licious*. Not being a size five never stopped her from thinking, or letting everyone else know, that she was the hottest and sexiest thing on the planet. She was slightly "plump," but not fat. "How much did *these* set you back?" she chimed in.

Brenda raised her eyebrows, laughed, then grabbed a yogurt from the frig. "You don't want to know. Trust me."

"That's the *third* new pair you've worn this week, isn't it?" Tessa wasn't a tomboy. She enjoyed looking feminine, yet she saw no good reason to spend a fortune on shoes like that.

Brenda's fantasy was to acquire as many as Imelda

Marcos someday. And these were not any run of the mill kind of shoes. Her closet held mostly four-inch spiky heels in every color of the rainbow, several from the collections of the most famous and expensive designers, including Jimmy Choo and Manolo.

"Yes, it is." Brenda lifted her chin defensively. "But that's why I work, girls," she said with a wink, "to feed my addiction." With that, she turned and sashayed in the direction of her office, clicking her way back down the tiled hall.

ᖰᖱᖰ

Later over lunch, the three friends discussed getting together on the weekend. Michelle thought snorkeling sounded like fun. Brenda, of course, mentioned shopping, and Tessa brought up hiking. Nobody could come up with a plan they could agree on. After tossing around a few other ideas that were quickly vetoed by one or the other, the women stared down at their food. They wracked their brains to come up with other options that might appeal to them all.

Michelle stood and threw her take out container in the trash. When she walked by one of the bulletin boards, her eyes lit up. Sitting back down next to her friends, she pointed at a flyer advertising bus tours around Waikiki. "How about going to the beach?"

The other two shrugged, well aware of the motive

behind this suggestion. Brenda rubbed a hand up and down her arm. "I guess I could use a little color, my tan is starting to fade."

Tessa nodded. "Sounds good. It would give me a chance to relax and finish the book I'm reading. I'll also text Veronica and see if she can get away from the spa for a few hours."

ↄ҉ↄ

Around ten o'clock the next morning, the four friends arrived at the beach to soak up the warm, tropical sun; enjoy the gentle, ocean breeze; and spend some quality girl-time together. Well, at least that was the intention of *three* of the women. Michelle was a huge flirt and always on the prowl for new, hunky beefcake to ogle. While Brenda, Veronica, and Tessa relaxed in lounge chairs, reading books and magazines, Michelle freely expressed her appraisal of the men who happen to stroll by. Wolf whistles and comments like, "Hey sexy, why don't you bring those six-pack abs over here?" filled the air. Several were accompanied by a wide grin and a flirty wink. Other beach goers scowled in their direction every time she yelled out a comment about a good-looking male and his physique.

Michelle was a short, compact bundle of dynamite. What she lacked in height, she made up for in a sassy and spunky attitude. Her father was originally from the mainland, and she was a "mini-me" of her native Hawaiian mother in her exotic looks.

The four friends had been there about an hour when two well-built specimens jogged by, probably local Marines by the looks of their haircuts.

In an instant, Michelle jumped up and started chasing after them, arms waving in the air above her, trying to get their attention. "Wait up guys! Hey, where are you going?"

Hiding behind their reading materials, the remaining women slumped down in their chairs, pretending that the crazy person running down the beach was not a part of their group.

A moment later, Brenda risked a peek over her latest issue of *Cosmo*. "Oh no," she whispered loudly, a mixture of concern and embarrassment in her tone.

"What happened?" Tessa and Veronica said in unison, scanning the area around them wondering what might have caused such a reaction.

"One of Michelle's flip flops just flew off and hurled through the air. It barely missed hitting the little girl in the pink and yellow swimsuit over there."

Tessa and Veronica followed the direction of Brenda's gaze. They were just in time to see the child's mother fling the sandal away while yelling some not-so-lady-like comments at Michelle. Apparently, the woman considered the harmless piece of rubber an imminent, life-threatening danger to her daughter.

Michelle continued on her mission, staggering in the deep, loose sand, sending a fine layer over the sunscreen-coated skin of the other beach goers in her pursuit of the hunks. All at once, the other three women broke out in a chuckle. A small breeze caused their friend's floppy hat to become airborne. It dipped and floated here and there on the gentle current, finally coming to rest on the rotund, sunburned belly of a man who had fallen asleep.

Eventually, Michelle gave up the chase. After finding her wayward flip-flop, she successfully retrieved her hat without waking up the snoring tourist. Stumbling back to her friends, she plopped down on the empty beach chair. Dark brown, wavy hair stuck out all over from the beautiful braid she'd started the day with. Her face was red and perspiration glistened on her skin. Using a towel, she wiped her forehead, cheeks, and upper lip.

"Whew, it's hot—and that sand—is hard to run in—but I almost—caught 'em." She grinned, trying to catch her breath. "Oh well, their loss."

Three pairs of eyebrows rose simultaneously. Tessa, Brenda, and Veronica shook their heads, constantly surprised, even after all this time, by what their friend said and did. Life was always an adventure with Michelle around.

CHAPTER 4

It was a gorgeous Sunday afternoon at the beginning of September. Brenda and her husband, Mike, were having a barbeque at their house to celebrate the Labor Day weekend. Michelle was helping in the kitchen when Tessa arrived. The three of them had been busy yesterday making all the side dishes for the party. There was potato salad, macaroni salad, garden salad, cheesecake, double-fudge macadamia nut brownies, and pineapple upside down cake with fresh pineapple from the Dole farm on the island. Mike was in charge of grilling the hamburgers and hot dogs. Some of the men he worked with were bringing the sodas, beer, ice, and chips.

Unfortunately, Veronica and her family wouldn't be

able to attend because they were spending the next couple of days with Ruben's relatives on the other side of the island.

The three women carried the tablecloths, plates, and miscellaneous utensils outside to the folding tables. Some would be set up buffet style for the food and some had chairs placed on either side for people to sit down and eat.

Mike snuck up behind Tessa, placed his arm around her shoulders, and gave her a quick hug "Hey, beautiful."

They were very close, like brother and sister.

"Hey, yourself." When she turned, she saw someone else walk up next to him.

"Tessa, I'd like you to meet a friend of mine. This is Dylan Cooper. Coop, this is—"

Dylan smiled and offered his hand. "Ms. Matthews, it's nice to see you again."

Mike looked back and forth between them, confused. "You already know each other?"

"Mr. Cooper was the Good Samaritan who changed my tire a few weeks ago," she explained to Mike without looking at him.

When she accepted Dylan hand, sparks skittered up her arm forcing her to end the contact quickly. *What was that?* It didn't matter. She had no reason to believe she would be seeing him after today. *But then again, this was twice in a rather short amount of time.*

"And who is this?" Michelle butted into the conversation and edged her way up close to the tall stranger. Mike introduced her and she took her time looking him over from head to toe.

Tessa pulled on Michelle's arm. "C'mon, Brenda needs our help in the kitchen."

"Huh? I didn't hear her call us. You go ahead." She waved her fingers at Tessa. Giving Dylan a wide smile, she popped out a hip, rested one of her hands there, and gave him the once over, again. "I think I'd like to spend more time getting to know Dylan."

"Let's go," Tessa growled through gritted teeth and tugged harder on Michelle's arm.

Mike nudged his friend. "It's probably time we go get the coolers ready and check on the grill, don't you think, Coop?"

"Sure." Dylan followed Tessa with his eyes until she disappeared through the sliding glass doors. He was glad to see her again. He couldn't tell if she was uncomfortable having to admit they had met before or if there was another reason she seemed in a hurry to go inside. Her friend, on the other hand, was anything but subtle. "What's with that short one?"

Mike chuckled. "She's a little man crazy, but basically she's harmless. Be careful not to let her corner you alone in the dark. She'd climb you like a bear after honey."

Dylan scowled and Mike burst out laughing.

"You think that's funny, don't you? She may be little, but she scares me." Dylan shook all over as if he were suddenly hit by a cold gust of wind.

Once in the house, Michelle scurried over to Brenda. "Where have you been hiding that drop-dead gorgeous man? And why haven't you set me up with him?"

Brenda frowned. "Who?"

"That guy!" Michelle pointed vigorously out the kitchen window. "He's one big hunk of eye candy! Did you see the muscles on that mountain of testosterone?"

Brenda shrugged. "Dylan? He's all right, I guess."

"All right? Are you blind? Oh my goodness, I think I'm in love."

Brenda shook her head. "No, you're in lust, again. Besides, from what Mike says, he's quite the player and a confirmed bachelor with *lots* of girlfriends. He's always been polite to me, but I don't know how he treats the women he dates."

Michelle tipped her head slightly and nodded. "I'm okay with that. Who knows? Maybe I'll be the one to win his heart."

Tessa and Brenda looked at each other and rolled their eyes, leaving Michelle staring out the window. They walked over to the frig, pulling out a head of lettuce and couple of tomatoes for the burgers.

"Here, Michelle," Tessa said, "slice these up, please. Maybe it will help cool you off a little."

By four o'clock, the backyard was full of friends eating, laughing, and having a good time. Tessa noticed the single women who were there found lots of reasons to be where Dylan was. He didn't seem to mind all the attention. She had no doubt that he drew females to him like a magnet wherever he went, with very little effort on his part. He was clearly one of those men. Just then, he glanced her way and caught her looking at him. He gave her a sexy smile that she knew had been polished over time to flawless perfection. An embarrassed rush of color heated her cheeks. Tessa tried to avoid Dylan the rest of the party. If she noticed him walking in her direction, she would find an excuse to go somewhere else.

Later that evening after all the other guests had left, the remaining five got busy cleaning up the backyard. They put the leftovers in storage containers and re-sealable plastic bags to toss in the frig.

Dylan returned from taking two large, black garbage bags out to the dumpster when he spotted Tessa alone next to one of the tables. Now was his chance to talk to her. "Nice party."

She saw him coming out of the corner of her eye, but she couldn't make her escape in time. She didn't like being around him. He stirred things up in her that she preferred to leave buried. "Yes, it was."

"Would you like some help?"

"No, thanks. I've got it," she responded without facing him. Hopefully, Mike would need his assistance soon and he'd leave her in peace to finish washing down the white folding tables.

He rested a hip against the corner of the one she was cleaning. "I wish I'd had a chance to talk to you, though," he admitted, hoping to make up for lost time.

"You didn't seem to be suffering from loneliness, Mr. Cooper." Her voice held a hint of sarcasm. Inside, her stomach was fluttering and she prayed he would go away.

He chuckled. "What I can say? I guess they liked what they saw."

Tessa stopped and looked at him. She wanted to see if he was serious and that egotistically shallow, or if he was teasing her.

The minute she raised her eyes to meet his, he grinned and flexed a little to emphasize his last statement.

"Really? Is that how you pick up women?" She slid her index finger under the sleeve of his skin hugging T-shirt and gave it a tug. "Little tight, don't you think?"

"I'm flattered that you noticed. It shows off my muscles and the girls seem to like that."

"Exactly, and um, I don't see any of them still here." Craning her neck with exaggerated movements, she looked around the backyard and over her shoulders. "Didn't you find one that you liked?"

She wasn't like the women he usually dated. She stood up to him and challenged him. *This could be fun.* "I prefer my dates a little more classy and ladylike." He winked. "More like you."

"If you want to date a lady, you'll need to use a different kind of bait." When she saw a puzzled expression come over his face, she continued. "Try a size larger shirt. It will still show off 'your guns.'" She used her fingers and wiggled them in the air indicating quote marks. "But it won't look like you have a second job as a male stripper."

He ran his hand down over the fabric stretched across his chest and toned stomach. "I like my shirts this way."

"Suit yourself." She shrugged and turned to leave.

Dylan laughed. "No, wait. I was just messing with you. Hey, at least I got you to talk to me. And I enjoy talking to beautiful women."

She placed both hands on her hips, not amused by his flirting. "Wow, you really have your pick-up lines down, don't you?"

"It's not a line, Tessa." He stood, took a step closer to her. "If I wear a *proper* button-up shirt, will you go out with me next Saturday?"

His dark, chocolate brown eyes took her captive. She was paralyzed, like a deer caught in headlights. He made her feel strange and warm inside. Tessa needed to get away from him before she agreed to something she would regret. She shook her head to clear her brain. "No, I can't. Thank you for asking, Mr. Cooper."

She turned to bolt, but he gently caught her arm. "Why not? And please, call me Dylan. Is it because of the other women—"

"What? No, I—I just can't. I really need to go." Her head was spinning and she made her way into the house as quickly as she could without running.

Dylan stared after her. He wasn't used to being rejected. A few minutes later, Mike came outside. The two men collapsed the folding tables and inspected the backyard to ensure there wasn't any trash laying around. After they put the coolers, chairs, and tables in the garage, Dylan said his goodbyes to Brenda and Michelle. He didn't see Tessa.

Mike walked his friend out to the driveway and they stood there a few minutes discussing plans for a scuba diving trip they wanted to take. Dylan climbed into his truck, but before he left, he nodded toward the house. "What's the story with blonde?" he asked nonchalantly.

Mike glanced at the front door. "Tessa?" His eyes narrowed and his voice was gruff, as if it held a warning, "She's not your type."

Dylan raised a brow. "My type?"

"Yeah, I saw that look in your eye when I introduced you earlier. I've seen that look before. Forget it."

"What are you talking about?"

"She's not a love 'em and leave 'em kind of woman. She's sweet and kind. She's a lady. The kind you marry, not the kind you play with." Mike paused. "She went through a really rough time about a year ago."

Dylan nodded. "Yeah, she told me that her husband died over in 'the sandbox.' That's too bad."

Mike looked at his friend, puzzled, "She did? She doesn't really talk about Ben to strangers."

"After I finished changing her tire, I saw the bumper sticker and asked her about it. She didn't go into detail. All she mentioned was that he'd died while on deployment in Iraq. She seemed a little frazzled."

"She still has good days and bad days". Mike stared at Dylan. "Anyway, she's off limits. Understand?"

Dylan chuckled softly, reaching out of the truck window to slap his friend on the arm. "Don't worry, she's safe around me. Besides, who are you? Her body guard?"

"Actually, yeah. Self-appointed. You can have any other girl on the whole island, Dylan, but steer clear of Tessa."

A seriousness clouded Mike's face that Dylan hadn't seen before. He wouldn't give his word to stay away when something deep down inside made him believe he wasn't going to be able keep that promise. His curiosity was peaked. The Corps was a family. He understood that. However, Tessa was a big girl. What was it about her that Mike felt as if he needed to draw a hard line when it came to her?

Dylan always did love a challenge and Tessa Matthews sparked his interest.

CHAPTER 5

Tessa was up, dressed, and out of the house early for a Saturday. Inside those walls was the last place she wanted to be today. She drove around awhile with no particular destination in mind. Before long, she found herself at the ocean. She was drawn to it when her heart and thoughts were in turmoil. Walking along the beach, with the breeze caressing her face, she prayed it would miraculously carry away her overwhelming sadness and despair. She spotted a bench in a nearby park next to the wide sidewalk. She decided to sit and try to sort out the jumbled mess clogging her brain.

The bright rays of morning sun glistened off the gold band Tessa always wore on a long chain around her neck. It usually stayed hidden beneath the dress or shirt she was wearing. But now, she caressed it, sliding Ben's wedding ring from her thumb to her index finger as she stared, lost in thought, out at the varying shades of blue water.

The day she'd dreaded for the last couple of weeks had finally arrived. It had been a year ago that her world had been turned inside out. The details and the emotions, at least the ones she could remember, were as vivid as if they had happened yesterday. Others had been a little fuzzy, until Veronica explained them to her a few months later. As the haunting images flooded over her, Tessa shut her eyes tight against the pain and pressure building in her chest.

Early that life-changing morning, she'd planted a few flowers in the window boxes and was about to start painting the kitchen a cheery shade of light yellow. She'd wanted everything to be perfect when Ben came home next month. She had barely popped the top off the first can of Lemon Sunrise when there was a knock on the door.

"Coming." She was expecting Veronica, her best friend who had volunteered to help her, but the door must have been locked or she would have let herself in. "Sorry, I guess—"

Unfortunately, when she pulled on the knob, Tessa's gaze fell upon a pair of somber-looking men in uniform. She had been around the military long enough to know this wasn't a social call. It only took a split second for her to realize why they were there. She felt the color drain from her face, and she thought she was going to faint. Shaking her head, she backed slowly into the living room.

Pointing vigorously at them with her index finger, she shouted, "No! Don't you say it! Don't you dare say a damn thing!"

Her body trembled and her voice cracked. She'd comprehended the reason for their visit long before either man uttered a single word.

"I'm sorry, Mrs. Matthews," one of the men stated before they stepped into the house.

Tessa soon found the back of her legs pressed up against the sofa. Her knees gave out and she dropped down onto the cushion. She saw their lips moving and heard them talking, but absorbed very little of what they were trying to explain to her. Now shock had set in. It felt as if she were in a tunnel or a cave. Everything was distorted, her hearing, her vision. A moment later, Veronica showed up. She'd rushed to Tessa's side and placed a comforting arm around her friend's shoulder. Every so often, Veronica asked Tessa if she understood what the men were telling her.

Only bits and pieces made it through the fog. "Sorry for your loss...line of duty...sacrificed for his country...brave Marine...purple heart...Arlington."

After the men left, Veronica held Tessa as she sobbed, brokenhearted and inconsolable. Eventually, she raised her pleading eyes to meet her friend's.

"This can't be real. Please tell me this is just a nightmare and that I'll wake up. Please! This can't be happening."

Veronica's eyes were red from crying, too. "I wish I could. You don't know how much I want to tell you that this has all been a horrible mistake." She paused. "But I can't." Her voice was strained and barely above a whisper as she stared at Tessa. "Let me make you some tea. What you need right now is sleep. We can talk when you wake up. Do you still have any of those muscle relaxers from when you fell and hurt your back?"

Tessa was drained and felt a little like a zombie. Nodding, she let her friend lead her down the hall to the bedroom. Veronica pulled back the covers, slipped off Tessa's shoes, and helped her crawl under the sheet. Beyond that, her recollections were hazy, hit and miss, until she heard the rest of the story later. One of their friends worked at the clinic on base as a pharmacist. Veronica had made a quick call to confirm it was safe to give Tessa the prescription, especially under the circumstances. After hearing the horrible news, their friend had assured Veronica that one tablet would be fine, but encouraged her to contact a doctor if Tessa became too despondent.

Walking into the bathroom, Veronica had tapped one white pill into her palm from the brown plastic bottle she'd retrieved from the medicine cabinet. She carried the cup of tea to Tessa's bedside and stayed until her friend fell asleep.

Veronica had told her the first two phone calls she made were to Brenda and Michelle.

Several hours later, when Tessa woke up, blackness surrounded her. She'd felt numb and groggy. At first she was confused. *Why is it so dark in here? What happened? Why am I in bed?* She stumbled out of the bedroom door. A dim glow from the kitchen helped light her path down the familiar hallway. Plates, platters, bowls, and various casseroles of food covered the counter. She was startled to find Veronica sitting at the table, gripping a blue coffee mug, and staring intently into the dark liquid.

"What are you doing here?"

Veronica's weary expression and sad attempt at a smile had jolted Tessa's brain. Then she remembered. Reality slammed into her as a wave of overwhelming pain crashed against her. Pressing both palms down on the counter for support, she'd closed her eyes. "Oh God, it really happened, didn't it? It wasn't a nightmare was it?"

"No." An agonizing whisper escaped, as if the breath struggled to break free. "I'm so sorry." The sorrow and trembling in Veronica's voice only added to the impact of her friend's words.

Once again, Tessa's legs had refused to support her. She slid down the cabinets. Folding herself into a tight ball, she pressed her back and shoulders against the wooden doors.

Veronica went over, sat next to her on the floor, and

just stayed there. She held Tessa, tried to comfort her—
and cried with her.

That was the best she could do.

The only thing she could do.

Veronica hadn't said anything. There weren't any
words known to the English language that could alleviate
even an ounce of the pain Tessa was experiencing.

And they both knew it.

❧❧❧

Tessa was pulled from her thoughts by a sharp pain
in her hand. When she opened her eyes, the source was
immediately apparent. While her memories played out in
her mind, her grip on Ben's ring had increased, causing
deep indentations into her fingers and palm. A burning
lump lodged in her throat, making it hard to swallow. Her
heart felt as if it had been sliced open with a jagged piece
of broken glass.

The breeze brushed her cheeks again. Her skin felt
cool. It was damp from the tears that had escaped between her lashes as she recalled the events of that horrible
day. *If only I hadn't answered the door—*

She knew how ridiculous that sounded because the
men would have only come back later. She swiped at her
face then dug in her purse for tissues. Normally, she
would need the small compact mirror she always carried
with her, but she hadn't bothered to apply any make-up

this morning knowing there would be tears off and on all day.

Lots of tears.

Her heart was heavy, reliving the unbearable pain her flashback resurrected, and she could feel a migraine coming on. It was time to leave. But where? Home wasn't an option yet, she had no appetite, and she wasn't in the mood to deal with the crowds at the mall. She began walking in the direction of her car when all of sudden she heard someone call her name.

"Tessa? Tessa, is that you?"

She turned and saw a man running across the beach toward her. Dylan Cooper. Her shoulders sagged as she exhaled. *Not today. I don't need his egotistical, flirtatious bull.* Forcing a smile, she crossed her arms and waited for him to reach her. Good manners dictated she at least say hello. His dazzling smile was predictably in place.

"What brings you down to the beach?" he asked.

"Just felt like getting out of the house."

Dylan was a pretty good judge of people. He'd only met her a couple of times, but he wasn't buying that excuse. He noticed her touching a gold chain around her neck. It peeked his curiosity but he didn't ask. He nodded behind him at the sand. "I thought I'd go for a run before it got too crowded."

"I won't keep you then, Mr. Cooper. Have a good day." Tessa started to walk away, but Dylan fell into stride beside her.

"Actually, I'm done. Would you like to get a bite to eat? I'd have to shower first, obviously," he said with a chuckle.

"No, thank you. I'm not hungry and I really don't feel like talking. I need to go—"

"Wait. Have you been crying?" He sounded concerned.

But all Tessa heard was him trying to pry into her personal affairs. The question startled her. She hadn't guessed a man like Dylan would notice such things, especially since she had patted all the moisture off her eyes and face. She lifted her chin and the tone of her voice was abrupt. "That's none of your business. Now, if you don't mind, I'd like to be left alone."

He stopped and raised his palms in surrender. "Sure, no problem. I'll make sure I have my goose down jacket out of storage next time I talk to you. I wouldn't want to get frost bite," he snapped.

Tessa spun around to look at him. He'd picked the wrong day to mess with her. "Why do you care, anyway? Are you the Dr. Phil of Hawaii? What difference does it make to *you* if I've been crying or not?" Her emotions had been running so high all morning that one quickly bled into the other. Before she could argue any further, she felt tears burning in her eyes. She tried to stop them, but they refused to be restrained and rolled down her cheeks. "Now look what you've done!"

He frowned. "Excuse me? Tessa, what's going on?"

She didn't answer him at first. She didn't want him to know anything about her life, but then the words trickled out before she could stop them. "It was a year ago today that I found out my husband had been killed in Iraq."

Dylan felt like a jerk. "I'm so sorry, Tessa. Can I call you a cab or call Mike and Brenda to come pick you up? You're pretty upset and probably shouldn't be driving right now."

At first, she wasn't sure if she should hit him for trying to tell her what to do, thank him for his concern, or accept his apology. She immediately realized she didn't have the energy to carry out the first option, so she went with a combination of the other two. "I'll be fine. I appreciate the offer. I'll take a few minutes after I get into my car and wait until I'm okay to make it home. Goodbye, Mr. Cooper."

Before he could respond, Tessa turned and walked away.

This time without interruption.

CHAPTER 6

For what seemed like the hundredth time since leaving the dry cleaners a few minutes ago, Tessa re-positioned the wire hangers as she searched for a way to prevent the hooks from pressing painfully into her fingers. She was tempted to fling the garments into the crook of her elbow, but she didn't want to wrinkle them. Especially since she'd just spent more money than she'd thought was necessary to remove a few stains and press her work clothes.

She knew the thin, slick plastic would slip and slide around on her arm, anyway.

She shouldn't complain, she was thankful to have found a cleaners open on Sundays. She'd been shopping most of the morning and purchased a couple of new dresses to wear to the office, a new pair of tennis shoes, and a few other miscellaneous things.

She had one last stop to make before heading home, and she hoped it would be quick. Hesitating for a moment outside the store, she debated on whether to take what she had to the car and come back or stop at another location closer to the parking lot. After all, there was an ABC Store on almost every block. They reminded her a little of a Circle K or 7-11, but more diverse. They sold candy, soda, snacks, and beer. They also had souvenirs, T-shirts, and all kinds of different things. In hindsight, she should have made this her first stop.

Tessa didn't bother grabbing a cart on her way in because she only intended on picking up a couple of small items. But now, she was feeling overwhelmed in the back corner of the store. Things were stacked, cradled, and crammed into her arms wherever she could find a spot amongst the ever growing pyramid. She finally made her way to the register and had just finished paying when her cell phone chimed. Digging around in her handbag, she found it and answered it before the call went to voice mail.

"Hey, Brenda." Tessa tucked it between her check and shoulder. She smiled and mouthed, "Thank you" to the cashier on her way out.

It was difficult trying to shove her wallet back into her purse, gather up her purchases, maneuver her slippery dry cleaning, and carry on a conversation with her friend.

Dylan was downtown looking for a birthday present for his mom He noticed a woman overloaded with bags step out of the corner store a few feet ahead him, but he couldn't see her face. The only view he had of her was from behind, and he liked what he saw. Dylan probably wouldn't have paid much more attention to her except he saw her walking toward the crosswalk, and the countdown on the display across the street was already blinking the number three. The rest of the pedestrians were almost to the other side when she stepped off the curb. Suddenly, he heard the roar of the engine a split second before he saw the car speeding toward the intersection.

Dylan bolted forward. "Ma'am! Look out!"

She didn't hear him. He grabbed her upper arms and jerked her backward just as the red, Corvette convertible raced past them.

Tessa screamed, thinking she was being attacked, but she didn't have time to fight. A heartbeat later, she realized what had happened. The phone flew out of her hand, landing on top of her dry cleaning bags, and she was sitting on the sidewalk next to them. She could hear Brenda's muffled voice, but another voice, a male voice, boomed closer.

Dylan knelt down next to her with one hand resting on her trembling shoulder. "Are you all right?"

Still stunned, Tessa held her hand against her forehead and nodded. "I think so." When she looked up, her gaze came to rest on the face of the handsome Marine.

"Tessa?" His eyebrows drew together, he couldn't believe it. "Are you hurt?" He wanted to make sure she hadn't twisted an ankle or had any other injuries as a result of him dragging her out of the road. "Sorry if I handled you a bit rough, but there wasn't time to be gentle."

The care and concern in Dylan's eyes was unnerving and something more than gratitude sparked inside of her. They stared at each other until she noticed people were beginning to gather around. A flush of embarrassment heated her face.

"I'm fine. Thank you. I—I didn't…" She waved in the direction of the street. A distant voice kept calling her name, and she realized it was coming from her phone. Picking it up she explained to Brenda what almost happened. "Yes, Dylan…Yeah, lucky, I know…I will… Bluetooth it is. I've gotta go, I'll call you when I get home." Tessa ended the call without waiting for any further response from her friend.

He witnessed a mixture of emotions sweep across her face. Shock and traces of fear lingered around her eyes as she continued to process the reality of the situation. Confusion was obvious by the lines on her forehead, questioning why he was there. But the one that tugged at his heart the most—a hint of pure vulnerability in the catch of her voice.

Dylan helped Tessa stand. They gathered all of her bags then he offered to walk with her to her car. She was shaken and didn't want to seem ungrateful, but she just wanted to go home. She managed a small smile. "I think I'll be fine. I appreciate the offer though."

He was disappointed, but not surprised. After talking to her at the barbeque and at the beach, he had discovered she was a strong, independent woman. Tessa preferred to handle things on her own. The day he had changed her tire was an exception. If her phone had worked, she would have called roadside assistance. She would have been in control of the situation, which was much different from feeling powerless and having to rely on the kindness of a stranger. Although she'd been polite, he now understood how helpless she must have felt. He would bet his last dollar she had hated that.

When Tessa started to walk away, she wobbled slightly. Dylan immediately went to her side and cupped her elbow. He nodded up ahead. "How about I buy you a cup a coffee? I was headed there right before I saw you," he lied skillfully.

He wanted to keep her pride intact, but he also knew she needed to sit awhile and recover from almost being run over. Even if it was her fault for not watching where she was going. However, he didn't think it was a good idea to mention that right now.

When she stopped and looked up at him, the answer was obvious. She should agree. But there was something about him that made her nervous. Her stomach twitched every time he smiled at her. Motioning with her arms, she replied, "I probably should be getting home. Even though

I'm very grateful for what you did, Mr. Cooper, remember what I told you at Mike and Brenda's. I'm not interested—"

"You know, I really wish you'd call me, Dylan. Mr. Cooper was my father and it makes me feel old when you say that." He placed his hand on her shoulder again and leaned in closer. "It's just coffee, Tessa. It's not a marriage proposal," he whispered with a playful smirk. Jiggling his eyebrows, he added, "But if you can spare a few minutes to keep me company, I'll spring for a dessert, too."

Her heart reacted to his teasing and she fought back a chuckle. He was charming, but deep down inside her instincts told her to run.

Run fast.

She didn't listen.

She felt on edge around him, and he brought out the "fight or flight" response in her. It didn't make sense, but maybe she was more shook up than she realized. The twinkle in his deep brown eyes brought an unexpected smile to her lips. "All right—Dylan." His hand remained where it was, and she didn't pull away. "Actually, a cup of tea sounds wonderful. Thank you."

Without asking again, he grabbed the dry cleaning and a couple of the shopping bags from her before they continued on their way.

He held the door for her and they took their place in line at the counter. After ordering, they found an empty table by the window where pleasant small talk filled the minutes while they enjoyed the delicious sweets and sipped their coffee and tea.

About an hour later, Tessa regretted her decision. Agreeing to join him had been a mistake. They were in public and it was just two people talking together. But her pulse skittered through her body at his laugh faster than she wanted it to.

Her fingers automatically searched out her gold chain. She found the feel of it calming in stressful or uncomfortable situations.

"That must be special to you?" Dylan casually pointed at her hand. "I noticed you touching it when I changed your tire and that day at the beach."

Tessa's fingers fumbled slightly. She didn't know if she wanted to talk to him about Ben. Maybe getting it out in the open would let him know where she stood and why she wouldn't date him. "Yes, it is. It's my husband's wedding band. I feel close to Ben when I wear it." She paused. Emotions squeezed tight around her heart. "I love and miss him very much."

"I have friends that have gone through the same thing. It's very sad. I'm sure it's been difficult being alone all this time." An awkward silence surrounded them, causing the space to feel cramped and crowded, even at a table for four. "You're so young to be a widow."

Dylan stared at the ring and then up into her eyes,

but didn't say anything for a minute or so. Mike had warned him she was off limits, but he didn't always do what he was told. "Ben was a lucky man, Tessa." He paused again. There was something he wanted to ask her. His hesitation wasn't because of the question, but the timing. In the end, as usual, he laid his cards on the table. "Would you like to go out to dinner sometime?"

At first, she blushed at the complement then alarm sirens blared in her head. "You mean like a date?"

He smothered the laugh that hovered on his lips. "That's what the kids are calling it these days, or so I'm told."

Amusement once again danced in his eyes, and she thought he was making fun of her, but she didn't find it funny at all. He caught her off guard, and she wrapped her fingers around the empty cup in front of her, "No, thank you."

"Do you have a boyfriend?"

"No."

"Do you usually eat dinner?"

"Yes, most of the time."

"So you just don't want to have dinner with *me*?"

"Right."

A slight twitch appeared at the corner of his mouth. He was enjoying this cat and mouse game he'd started.

"Would you rather go to the movies?"

Tessa scowled at him. "No." Her frustration escalated. "I don't date much," she said, her heartbeat increasing with each additional prying question. Why was he being so persistent? She shouldn't have agreed to this in the first place. She should've listened to that small voice that tried to warn her. "And, you may as well know, before your game of twenty questions continues, I refuse to date a Marine. It's nothing personal. It's just how it is," she stated matter-of-factly.

Frown lines appeared on Dylan's forehead. "Why? We're not all bad," he said with an easy grin.

She leaned forward and her eyes narrowed as she gave him the answer he was so determined to discover. "I don't see how that is any of your business. But, I doubt you'll give up until I tell you." Her chest began to ache as she recalled those first few months. "After my husband passed away, it was the worst time of my life. The pain was unbearable. I swore I'd never let myself get involved with any man in the military and put myself in a situation like that again. Ever."

"So you're telling me that because he died while serving in the Corps, you automatically rule out all the rest of us?" He hurried to clarify what he said after seeing the anger flash in her blue eyes. "I'm not making light of your loss, so please don't misunderstand. Mike told me a little about your husband, and he sounds like a great guy. It seems to me he wouldn't want you to hide in the past. He'd want you to live your life and move forward. Am I right?"

He immediately knew he'd crossed the line by the expression on her face.

Heat flared up in her, anger simmering just below the surface, and although her words were spoken softly, there was no mistaking how she felt. "You didn't know Ben, and I would appreciate you not telling me what *he* would want me to do with *my* life. I will date, or not date, whomever I choose, Mr. Cooper. I do not need, or want, your approval or opinion on the subject. Do I make myself clear?"

Dylan's face stung from the verbal slap as much as if she had reached across the table and hit him with her hand. He should respect her wishes, but he couldn't stop his mouth from adding fuel to the fire. He kept the tone of his voice as calm as he could, yet he was doubtful she would notice. Resting his forearms on the table, he leaned toward her. "Fine, but giving someone else a chance to make you happy won't diminish the love you had for Ben. You deserve to be happy again, Tessa. So when you're ready to join the land of the living, you let me know." His steady gaze never left hers as he sat back in his chair. He could tell he had hit a nerve.

Tessa wasn't going to stay there any longer and listen to this blowhard. "Goodbye, *Mr*. Cooper." She scooted her chair back, grabbed her dry cleaning, her purchases, and hurried out the door.

Dylan knew he should apologize, but he was fairly certain she wouldn't listen to anything else he had to say.

When he got up to leave a couple of minutes later, he noticed she'd forgotten one of her shopping bags. Slipping his fingers through the handles, he left the café. He knew she couldn't have gone very far. There. She was about a block away, so he took off in her direction. "Tessa! Tessa, wait."

Mad didn't even begin to describe how she felt. Gritting her teeth, the scene from a moment ago played over in her mind. *I should've punched him*! But because they were in a public place, she'd refrained. Suddenly, a hand touched her arm and it startled her. When Tessa spun around, she couldn't believe her eyes. Her response was sharp and immediate. "What do you want? Did you think of more pearls of wisdom you feel the need to share with me on how I should live my life according to the Book of Cooper?"

Dylan knew not to smile, but it was difficult. "No. You forgot this." He handed her the bag. "And I do want to say that I'm sorry. I shouldn't have said those things to you."

Lifting her chin, her steely eyes glared at him, "So you admit that you were wrong and out of line for talking to me that way?"

"Yes and no. I stand by what I said. I just shouldn't have judged you on how you chose to *not* live your life. I didn't mean to upset you."

"That's not exactly an apology," she challenged him.

"It's the best I can do."

She didn't detect any teasing in his eyes or sarcasm in the tone of his voice. He appeared to be sincere. Despite the fact that she was still mad, he had been thoughtful enough to bring the shopping bag to her. Tessa didn't have the energy to fight with him anymore today. Releasing a weary sigh, she responded, "Thank you for bringing my shoes. Good-bye, Mr. Cooper." Then she walked away.

After she left, Dylan went to his truck and sat there for several minutes, just thinking. He wondered what made him say those things to her. He had no idea. Why was he so concerned about this woman who had built a wall around herself that would rival the one in China? It was more than her beauty. He had dated his share of gorgeous women. There was just that unexplainable something that intrigued him, and he wanted to get to know her. He chuckled to himself because his chances of that happening didn't look too good right now. But something in the back of his mind made him believe he would have another chance, and he better not blow it. With a shake of his head, he turned the key and drove back to base.

Later that evening, Tessa replayed her encounter with Dylan. Static seemed to buzz through the air whenever he was around. She found his presence very unsettling. The way the gold flecks in his eyes appeared to sparkle a little brighter when he teased and flirted with her. And the easy way he could get her to smile, even when she tried not to. There was also the conversation she'd had with him at the coffee shop. He was wrong to talk to her that way, but at least he was honest about how he felt. While she was thinking about him, her shoulder began to tingle where he'd touched her twice today. Once out of concern and once in jest. Still, it only reinforced her resolve and the promise she had made to herself.

No Marines.

Not even a tall, handsome, brown-eyed one who made her laugh sometimes.

No. Especially not him.

CHAPTER 7

At work the next morning, the phone rang around ten o'clock. "Hello, Tessa Matthews."

"Hi. Do you have a minute to talk?"

Glad for a break from the computer screen, Tessa answered, "Sure, what's up?"

"I just heard what happened to you yesterday." Veronica's voice sounded concerned. "Are you all right?"

"I'm fine. It—wait." Tessa frowned. "How did you find out about it?"

"Brenda called and told me. I'm so glad Dylan was walking by."

There was no response, only silence.

"Hello? Are you still there?" Veronica asked to make sure she hadn't lost the connection.

Tessa doodled on a piece of scratch paper next to her keyboard. "I'm here. I just don't want to talk about him."

"Why? What did he do? Besides save your life."

Knowing her friend would not let the subject alone, Tessa recapped the conversation from the coffee shop. Even though Veronica couldn't see what was going on, Tessa emphasized certain details, using the pencil she held tightly in her fingers. She twirled it, poked the air with it, and jabbed at the scribble pad with it. "Can you believe he actually talked to me like that?"

Veronica was the one Tessa could always trust. She had been there with her through thick and thin. When there wasn't an immediate response to her question, Tessa knew her friend was thinking of a good way to tell her something she didn't want to hear.

"I understand that he doesn't know you well enough to be so blunt, but I agree with some of what he said."

There it was. "Really? Thanks a lot."

"Tessa, you should start dating again. When was the last time you allowed a man to take you out to nice restaurant or to the movies?"

"Well…a couple of weeks ago, that guy, Mark, and I went to eat at the new Sushi place down the street."

"That doesn't count."

"Why not?" Tessa protested.

"He's your cousin's husband who was in town on business," Veronica scolded.

Tessa cringed. She'd forgotten that she had told her

friends about him being her relative. "Well—I—ah—I have a date this weekend with a man named Trent. He's a financial advisor who works in my building."

She jotted a quick note to call him and accept his invitation to dinner. He'd asked her this morning in the elevator, and before she could give him an answer, Trent's boss called him on his cell. But now, she *had* to agree to go.

"Why didn't you tell me?" Veronica's voice took on an air of excitement.

"Because, I didn't want you all to hound me for days with a bunch of questions." She paused. "So see, I date," she announced triumphantly.

Veronica chuckled. "Whatever you say, girlfriend." There was silence again for a moment before she continued, because she already knew the answer. "But you won't consider going on a date with Dylan?"

Tessa didn't hesitate. The one-syllable word closed the door on any further discussion. "No."

☙☙☙

Saturday night, Tessa met Trent at the restaurant. She wasn't comfortable giving out her address to just any one. They sat and talked awhile before placing their order. She had been nervous, but Tessa was enjoying herself more than she thought she would. Trent was attractive, well-dressed, had a great job, and a good sense of humor. The food surpassed the critics reviews and the dessert was deliciously decadent.

They were enjoying their coffee, when out of the corner of her eye, she saw a familiar face. Dylan Cooper. A statuesque blonde stood next to him.

His eyes met Tessa's and he lifted a hand to wave.

At first, all she could do was stare then she started to get upset. Ridiculous at it was, she somehow believed he had plotted to come here tonight intending to irritate her. She realized that was absurd. He had no way of knowing her plans. Trent must have seen a change in her face when she watched Dylan and his date walk away.

"…Tessa?" Trent said. "Tessa, are you all right?"

"I'm—I'm fine. Just thought I saw someone I knew." She tried to play it off as nothing, hoping he would buy her excuse since he didn't know her very well.

"Are you sure? You're face went pale then your cheeks changed to a dark pink color, like you had been sunburned."

He looked concerned, and she thought that was sort of sweet.

"No, it's nothing."

But as soon as she said that, she turned her head to look at a nearby painting. What she found was Dylan and his date sitting only a few tables away.

After dinner, Tessa and Trent walked through a nearby pair of glass doors leading to an upscale bar area. There was a small dance floor, but no jukebox or DJ. The mellow music flowed from speakers placed around the room and the songs were pre-selected by management. They settled into a quiet booth. Trent ordered a martini and Tessa ordered a white wine. Their topics of conversation varied from family to sports to work. She didn't dwell on the details of Ben's death, and he didn't ask.

Tessa was about to excuse herself to use the ladies room when someone stopped next to their table. When she looked up, it was Dylan and the beautiful woman he came in with. A charming smile lit up his face like a shiny new penny.

"Good evening, Tessa. You look beautiful tonight, as always."

"Mr. Cooper." She saw a hint of amusement in his dark eyes at her formal response. He seemed to take great pleasure in teasing her. She and Dylan introduced their dates. Handshakes and "Hellos" were exchanged between them.

"I'm so glad I ran into you tonight. I wanted to stop by and ask your opinion on my new shirt." He feigned concern as he slid his hands down the sleeves and front of the mint green, button-up. "I value your fashion sense, and I think this is what you had in mind the last time we discussed my wardrobe choices. Right?"

The way Dylan was facing the table, nobody but Tessa saw the devilish wink he gave her. He was mocking her because she had made the comment about his T-shirts being too tight. She saw Trent looking back and forth between her and Dylan, confused by the conversation. Dylan's attempt to embarrass her in front of another man was an obvious sign of jealousy, especially since she had turned *him* down at the cafe.

Tessa believed he wasn't told "no" very often. Her anger flared again, and the hand that lay in her lap was clenched into a tight fist. "It looks fine, Mr. Cooper."

"Good." He beamed, pretending that getting her stamp of approval was a great relief to him. "I was hoping you'd like it. I didn't want to disappoint you."

"I think he looks very handsome," the other woman cooed, running her hand up and down his arm.

"There you go. Your lady friend approves and that's all that really matters. So you have a nice evening."

He was being dismissed. Dylan saw Tessa attempt to smile, but her eyes were hard as steel. He had taunted her on purpose and received the reaction he thought he would. She was feisty. She didn't fall all over him like most of the women he knew. She was riled up, and he took some weird satisfaction in that. It gave him the answer he was looking for. If she wasn't interested or attracted to him at all, his presence here tonight wouldn't have bothered her. But it *had* affected her.

Now he focused his attention back to the gorgeous model hanging onto his left arm. She was all about having fun. And that was exactly what he intended to do. "Goodnight, Ms. Matthews." With that, Dylan and his date walked away.

"Are you a fashion consultant, too?" Trent asked sincerely after the other couple left.

"No, he was…well, he…" Tessa shook her head. "Never mind, it's a long story." She had no intention of explaining it to him.

❧❀❧

Later when Tessa was getting ready for bed, she couldn't get the image of Dylan out of her mind. The way the light green fabric stretched across his broad shoulders and muscular chest made her forget about Trent. In fact, after Dylan arrived, the evening had gone downhill. She was either so focused on being mad at him for showing up at the restaurant or busy admiring the way he looked when he stopped only inches from her at the table in the bar.

Stop it! *This is crazy*! Trent was a perfectly nice man. If he called, she would agree to go out with him again—even if there were no sparks when he softly kissed her goodnight.

She had to stop thinking about Dylan Cooper.

There was no place for him in her future.

CHAPTER 8

Brenda and Mike, along with several of his buddies and their wives or girlfriends, met at the park to play a game of flag-football. When Tessa, Veronica, and Michelle arrived, most of the others were already there. A couple of the wives waddled across the grass with round, pregnant bellies encased in flowing sundresses. They eased themselves down into collapsible, canvas chairs and relaxed in the shade ready to cheer on their husbands. At the edge of the park, three squealing toddlers were whisked off to the adjacent kid's playground by their mothers.

Of course, everyone who knew Michelle made sure to remind her that tackling was not allowed. She could only grab *flags*, not butts. Rolling her eyes, she released a frustrated sigh. "You guys are a bunch of party-poopers. How's a girl supposed to have a little fun?" When her friends turned around, Michelle stuffed most of the red flag inside the front of her shirt. "How's this?" she inquired playfully as she wiggled her eyebrows and shimmied her chest.

"Don't even think about it." Brenda snatched the cloth and handed it to her friend. "Behave."

After the other three women walked away, Michelle tried another tactic to ensure physical contact with some of the good-looking men. Pushing the flag all the way down into one of her back pockets with just a tiny triangle poking out, she stubbornly lifted her chin. "I'll show these ol' fuddy-duddies how to make this game more interesting."

Dylan didn't show up until after the teams were chosen. That was when Tessa found out he'd been promised a spot on the opposing side. She watched him jog toward the rest of the group, his strong calves flexed below knee-length athletic shorts. He had on a drab, olive green T-shirt, like the ones Marines wore when they exercised, but he'd cut off the sleeves. She was thankful it wasn't as tight as the ones he'd worn to change her tire or to the barbeque. Tessa found the sight of him definitely unnerving with his muscles exposed and on display. Her heart began to beat a little faster and she didn't appreciate its betrayal of her common sense.

Dylan spotted Tessa and was happy she was playing

today. This would give him a chance to get a little more "up close and personal" with her during the game. Her blonde hair was drawn up into a ponytail, and pulled through the opening in the back of her pink cap. It matched the pink and gray, baseball style, T-shirt she wore. One end of the red, cloth flag was tucked into the right, back pocket of her denim, cut-off shorts. The other end draped over the sensual curve of her behind. His eyes continued downward to her lean, tanned legs that disappeared into white tennis shoes.

Gary's voice suddenly rang in Dylan's ears. "Earth to Dylan—Hello?"

"Oh—uh, hey. Everybody ready to go?"

"What's wrong with you?"

Slapping his friend on the back, Dylan smiled. "Just enjoying the view, dude. Just enjoying the view."

"I should've guessed," Gary admitted with a shake of his head as he followed his friend to the benches at the side of park.

Basic rules of the game were reviewed for the newbies before the yellow and blue mesh vests were handed out to designate the two teams.

After examining the flimsy "shirt," Carl piped up, "What's up with these? We always play shirts and skins."

Everyone looked at him as if he had just sprouted two heads.

"There are women playing today, you moron," Mike scowled.

Carl suddenly realized what he'd said. Without uttering another word, he pulled the mesh covering over his head, stepped off to the side, and waited.

Dylan turned his gaze on Tessa. "I guess we could consult with the girls. Which would you like to be, Tessa? Shirts or skins?" he asked. His teasing produced a slight twitch at one corner of his mouth.

She folded her arms across her chest. "You're a real comedian, aren't you, Mr. Cooper?"

"Well, if you want *my* opinion," Michelle chimed in with an eager grin as she assessed each of the male players. "I think *all* the guys should be skins."

"That's a shocker," Veronica muttered.

"*What*?" Michelle shrugged, her palms up toward the sky. "I thought this game was supposed to be fun."

As each team huddled together to discuss their strategies for victory, a slight breeze filtered through the surrounding trees. The warmth of the sun enhanced the sweet smell of the recently mowed grass. Dylan and Tessa lined up for the first play of the game. She stared straight ahead, refusing to look over at him, even though he was only a couple of feet away. He stirred things up in her that she didn't want to feel.

Midway through the first half, the score was tied. There had been a couple of turnovers and two touchdowns for each team. After one play, Dylan ran up behind Tessa. He grabbed her around the waist and tossed her gently down to the ground.

Shocked by the surprise attack, she shrieked. A second later, she was flat on her back staring up at sinfully sexy eyes. He'd pinned her arms next to her head against the soft grass, his body half covering hers. Boos and jeers could be heard in the background from the other players.

"Hey, this is supposed to be *flag* football, not *tackle*," she objected as forcefully as she could while his seductive gaze caressed her face.

She could feel the heat from his body through their clothes. The air between them sparked with electricity.

Some of Tessa's honey-blonde strands from her ponytail splayed across the back of his right hand. They felt like silk threads against his skin. Thoughts of running his fingers through her hair and letting it cascade between them sent a rush of want though him. His plan might be backfiring. He had set out to tease her, but now, he found himself sincerely captivated by her. A deep, husky laugh rumbled in Dylan's chest.

"Sorry, my mistake." He leaned down closer, his lips almost touching hers. "Some rules are just made to be broken, Tessa."

Her pulse thundered in her ears. Before she could catch the breath that had rushed from her lungs at the thought of him kissing her, he stood and held out his hand. Rising up on her elbows, she aimed a defiant glare at him for a moment before ignoring his offer. She rose to her feet without his help and brushed her hands across the back of her shorts to remove any dirt or grass. When a good comeback popped into her head, she spun around, only to see him walking toward his teammates without so much as a glance back over his shoulder.

After that, Michelle tried to get Dylan's attention. Finally, she maneuvered her way close to him. "You can tackle me anytime, hot stuff. And we can make it look like an accident."

Her smile stretched across her face like a hungry dog eyeing a T-bone steak. He ignored her. Disappointed, she went in search of a new victim. On the next play, she lined up facing one of the cute single Marines she'd seen at Brenda's house the day of the barbeque. "How do *you* feel about following these crazy rules that say we can't tackle?"

A look of panic flashed in the young man's eyes. But before he could answer, the football was thrown deep, and the other players left Michelle standing there, her intended prey far down the park.

As the game progressed, Dylan continued to flirt with Tessa. A part of him took great pleasure in making her squirm.

By half-time, the temperature was hovering around eighty-five. The teams were on the sidelines rehydrating with their beverage of choice.

All of a sudden, a loud gasp came from someone inside Tessa's group. When people turned to investigate, they discovered that it was Michelle, and she had her hand over her heart.

"What's wrong?" Brenda asked with Tessa and Veronica standing right beside her.

All three women looked at each other, wondering if Michelle was suffering from heat stroke or over excursion. It only took a moment for them to remember the most strenuous things she'd done all day was ogle and flirt with the unattached male players.

"Wrong?" Michelle responded in a rather trance-like tone. "Absolutely nothing. In fact, I think we should do this every weekend."

"What are you talking about?" Tessa said, slightly confused. "You don't even like football."

"Oh, I have recently become quite fond of the sport. I've decided that it's the best game ever invented." Another gasp from Michelle prompted her friends to inch closer. "Oh my gosh, I think I've died and gone to heaven. Hunk heaven." The others looked in the direction of Michelle's unwavering stare. At that moment, the other women understood the *problem* with Michelle.

With all the running around, several of the men had peeled off their shirts that were now drenched with sweat. Most of them were pouring water over their heads to cool off. It cascaded down their rippling torsos causing their tanned bodies to glisten in the midday sun.

Brenda planted her hands on her hips. "Seriously, Michelle?"

"You had us worried, don't do that again," Veronica scolded.

"I need something to drink," Michelle said, fanning herself by tugging on the V-neck of her shirt. "Man, it's really getting hot out here."

Tessa hated to admit it, but she couldn't stop her eyes from drifting over every inch of the man that had annoyed her all day. His tight shirts had left little to the imagination, but Dylan's bare chest triggered something. A ripple of attraction rushed through her. He caught her staring and flashed one of his intoxicating smiles at her. Blushing slightly, she turned away and grabbed a few ice cubes from the nearby cooler. She rubbed them against her throat and the back of her neck. The cold felt soothing on her warm skin.

She was acutely aware that it wasn't only the weather and the exercise that had forced her body's temperature to rise.

The third quarter was well underway when Tessa caught a pass and ran ten yards for a touchdown. Her laughter and excitement vibrated through the air. Dylan's heart beat faster as he watched her jump up and down while performing a silly victory dance. This playful side of Tessa made her even more appealing to him, especially compared to some of the high-maintenance women he occasionally dated.

Feeling especially mischievous today, he grinned while plotting his next scheme. Truthfully, he just wanted an excuse to touch her again—knowing it would probably irritate her was just an added bonus.

As Tessa trotted by, he slapped her on the butt and winked. "Good catch."

She saw a flicker of amusement dance in his dark eyes. The unexpected gesture startled her, and she almost tripped over her own feet. What was it about this man? He'd teased her all day like Bobby Watson used to back in the first grade when he'd pulled on her pigtails every chance he got. Even though Dylan's antics were annoying, they also made her feel beautiful and desired. But she didn't want *him* to be the man who aroused those feelings inside of her—she couldn't let that happen.

Unable to stop the tingling sensations spreading through her derriere, Tessa decided enough was enough. "Okay, tough guy. You wanna play? It's on," she whispered to herself on the way back across the grass to join her teammates.

The game was almost over, and she thought the time was right to show this macho Marine who he'd been messing with. A pass was headed straight for him and, when he was about to catch the football, she shoved him. He fell hard on his back in the wet, muddy grass where the guys had poured water over themselves earlier. Resting her hands on her hips, she leaned over slightly. Her sparkling blue eyes glared down at him, a triumphant smirk playing across her lips.

"Oops," she announced sarcastically. "Sorry about that, I guess some rules *are* made to be broken, Mr. Cooper."

As she jogged away, he closed his eyes. A hearty laugh escaped through his lips. *Tessa Matthews is a woman who knows how to hold her own.*

"Oh my goodness! Are you all right?" When he opened his eyes, Michelle was hovering over him, like a buzzard over a fresh kill. "Is anything broken?" She slid her hands up and down his arms and, of course, she couldn't resist touching his chest. "Maybe you need a little mouth to mouth to get some air back in your lungs."

The look of eager anticipation in her eyes forced Dylan to think fast. "No. That's okay, thanks. I'm fine." He scrambled to his feet before she could lock lips with him, offering her version of *help*.

☙❧☙

Dylan, Tessa, Michelle, Mike, Brenda, and about six other people went out for pizza at a local sports bar after the game. They ate, talked, and laughed. When some of them had finished eating, they drifted over to play darts or to challenge a friend to a game of pool. Veronica didn't join them. She wanted to stop by the spa and see how business had been today.

Michelle decided she'd find a willing instructor to teach her to play one of the indoor sports. It didn't matter that she already knew how. Others stayed behind at the tables just chatting or watching one of the many big-screen TVs hanging on the walls.

Tessa was answering a post on Facebook when she felt the chair next to her slide backward. Looking over, she expected to see one of her two best friends, but to her surprise, she found Dylan occupying the spot.

"Hey, why are you sitting over here all alone?"

She tapped her phone with her fingernail. "I'm checking my messages."

He jerked his thumb over his left shoulder, "I just got beat at darts. Oh, well, that's okay because I wanted to talk to you for a moment anyway."

Tessa eyed him. "Oh?"

"Before you say no, hear me out." He grinned. It was one of those impish smiles. The kind that reminded her of a little boy trying to talk himself out of getting into trouble with his mom. "I know you've made it very clear that you don't want to date a Marine. However, I was wondering if you would like to go to the Marine Corps Ball with me, as a friend. That wouldn't be breaking your rule, and I think we could have a really nice time."

Tessa stared at him for a few seconds before answering. "Thank you, but, I…um…"

"Mike and Brenda will be there if that will make you feel more comfortable."

His eagerness to sell her on this idea made her want to tease him a little.

"Don't you have enough women from your little black book at your beck and call, Mr. Cooper?"

Dylan chuckled. "Now, hold on. I didn't say I

couldn't get a date. Far from it. I just want to go and have fun. No expectations at the end of the night. No strings attached. Nothing more, nothing less."

Plucking a black olive off her slice of pizza, Tessa popped it into her mouth. She did miss going to the ball, but she hardly knew him. Could she trust Dylan's motives? Was it because he was handsome—and had a smile that should be considered illegal in all fifty states—that, when he was around, she experienced the flutters and tingles of attraction? Would it make her think about Ben? It was probably best to play it safe. "I do appreciate you asking, but no thank you, Dylan."

For a moment, he thought she was going to accept. But in the end, she allowed her fear to win again. He was disappointed.

Tessa's tone had been soft. She hadn't snapped at him or been harsh. That gave Dylan hope. Maybe he had a chance to get to know her yet. Slow and cautious. She was scared and would run if he didn't play his cards right. That was okay, he knew how to wait.

And something in him said Tessa was worth waiting for.

CHAPTER 9

Tessa couldn't think of a worse time for her air conditioner to go out. Her head pounded, her nose was stuffed up, and every muscle in her body ached. Wadded up tissues lay scattered across her floral comforter and on the floor next to her bed, like giant un-melted snowflakes.

"Oh, God, just take me now," she mumbled with the side of her face half buried in her scrunched up pillow. She might be running a fever, but she couldn't be certain because the room was so stuffy. And right now, she was too sick to go get the thermometer out of her medicine cabinet or to open the windows to see if there was a breeze.

Muffled noises down the hall broke the silence. She

thought about panicking for a split second, but realized she didn't have the energy.

A moment later, she heard someone call her name. "Tessa? We're here to fix you're A/C."

She rolled over onto her back and squinted through half-opened, bloodshot eyes. "Mike?" she moaned while trying to clear the fog from her brain. *How did he get in here?* Then she remembered that Brenda had a spare key to her house in case of emergencies.

Her bedroom door eased open slightly, and he peeked inside. "How are you feeling? Damn, you look like crap."

"Gee, thanks." She tried to make a sarcastic face at him, but her sinuses protested at the effort.

"Brenda sent over some soup in case you feel up to eating later. I stuck it in the frig."

Tessa nodded slightly in appreciation. Her thoughts drifted to something he'd said that puzzled her. "Did you say *we*? Who else is here?"

Jerking a thumb over his shoulder, Mike leaned his hip against the doorframe. "I brought Dylan with me."

Her eyes flew open as she bolted upright. A stabbing pain pierced her head. She grimaced and placed a palm flat on her forehead. "*What*? Don't you dare let him in here!" she warned while grabbing for a tissue barely in time to catch a body-jolting sneeze.

"Okay, okay. Just lay back down and rest. I don't see what the big deal is. He's been to war zones before, and he's seen a lot worse. Well, then again, I don't know, you do look pretty tore up," he smirked, teasing her.

"Get out." She tried to shout, but her head still hurt too much from her recent sudden movements.

"Fine, we'll try to get the air fixed as quickly as we can."

Tessa could hear him chuckling as he closed the door. With a groan, she pictured Mike's face and punched her pillow with what little energy she had. She would've killed him if he had let Dylan in her bedroom, allowing him to see her in this condition. She eased back down on the mattress, letting her lashes float closed.

Dylan walked up behind his friend. "What's so funny?" He'd been busy bringing in the rest of the tools from his truck and missed the conversation.

"Tessa's really sick and she didn't want you to see her like that." Mike rolled his eyes. "Women are so weird about things sometimes. I don't know why it matters."

Dylan understood, because he had two sisters. The men made their way back down the hall and headed outside.

Over the next couple of hours, they replaced the motor then cleaned and checked the entire A/C unit. They were almost finished when Mike's cell phone rang.

"Hello?...Now?...But..." His head fell forward and he exhaled. "Okay, I'll be right there."

Dylan looked at him. "What was that all about?"

"It was Brenda," Mike explained. "She's at some

fancy boutique down in Waikiki, and she wants me to come see a dress she found for the ball."

Dylan raised his eyebrows. "You're kidding, right?"

Mike shook his head. "No, unfortunately I'm not."

"So you're leaving? Just like that?"

"Someday you'll understand, dude. It means a lot to Brenda for me to come and see this dress. So I'm gonna go. Marriage is a give and take. If this little thing, no matter how crazy *I* think it is, will make her day, I'll gladly do it. She's put up with me being gone on training missions and away on deployment twice now. I figure it's the least I can do. I don't know what I did to deserve such a wonderful woman, and I don't ever want to think about what I'd do without her. I'll do anything to keep her happy."

Dylan had never seen this side of Mike before. He really loved and respected his wife. He truly cared about their marriage. Dylan had witnessed too many of his other friends screw up and lose what they had for stupid reasons.

"Speaking of the ball, have you found a date yet?" There was a trace of envy in Mike's voice as his mouth twitched in anticipation. He was happily married but still enjoyed living vicariously through his single friend who always had plenty of good-looking women chasing after him.

Dylan stalled. He didn't want to tell his buddy that he'd asked Tessa and she'd turned him down, so he played it off. "I'm narrowing down my options." A cocky grin lifted the corners of his mouth as he slapped his friend on the back. "Don't worry, you won't be disappointed."

"Someday a woman's going to tame you and your wild ways. I can't wait until you find that special person. One day she'll ask you to hold her purse at the mall, and you'll do it without giving it a second thought.

That woman might be closer than Mike thinks. But Dylan wasn't going to tell him that. Poking himself in the chest with his index finger, he continued their friendly male banter. "Never gonna happen. Not to this guy." Straightening, he lowered his hand. "I've still got a pair," he boldly responded, grabbing the crotch of his jeans. Both men cracked up at the testosterone driven gesture.

"We'll see," Mike challenged. "I said I'd never settle down, too—before I met Brenda."

One man knew the truth about the power of love and how it could change you. The other man didn't want to admit that he was beginning to realize that very same truth.

After Mike left, Dylan cleaned up the equipment and washed his hands. He latched the sliding glass door behind him and took the toolbox out to his truck. He was glad he'd brought his own vehicle instead of riding with his friend. Mike said he would flip the switch on the thermostat on his way out. Back inside the house, Dylan reached up and could feel the cool air flowing from the vent in the living room. It was obviously fixed. So why did he feel the need to go check on Tessa? Was it just because he wanted to defy her adamant request that he not go into her bedroom and see her in that condition? He had to admit he *was* a little curious to find out how bad she really looked. Or could the reason be that he was actually concerned about her and wanted to make sure she was okay? On his way down the hall, he decided the answer was a little of both.

When Dylan stuck his head into her room, he saw her lying there sprawled half in, half out of the covers. A leg here, an arm there. Even though he felt bad for her, he tried to hide his amusement. Her mouth hung wide open, her nose was red, and her blonde hair lay plastered against one side of her head. He took a moment to check the vent located on the wall across from her bed. It seemed to be working just fine. He stood there a little while longer and looked around the rest of the room, Tessa's room. Lace curtains framed two nice sized windows allowing lots of natural light to shine in. Several pictures in various sizes and frames hung on the walls. More sat clustered in groups on the tops of her two dressers and on the small table by the door. Dylan studied them, but only recognized a few people.

Some showed a little blonde girl and he could only assume it was Tessa when she was young, surrounded by her family.

Then his eyes fell upon a picture of a young, smiling

couple, and he knew right away that the man in the photo had to be Ben.

On the wall by the door hung their wedding picture. He'd worn his dress blue uniform and Tessa beamed with happiness, looking gorgeous in her flowing white gown. Dylan's chest felt tight. He needed to leave.

When he took one more look over his shoulder at her, he noticed the water glass on her nightstand was almost empty. *I should fill it up for her*. He crept over to her side of the bed, stopped, and gazed down at her. He smiled remembering Mike's assessment and had to agree. *Not her best look*. Still, the sight of her ignited things in him. She looked helpless, yet somehow alluring, and his protective instincts kicked in, right along with his desire for her.

She was wearing a yellow tank top and a pair of cut off, navy blue, sweat pants. They were short, exposing her tanned legs up to her hips. Although most of her chest was hidden under the pale lilac-colored sheet, he could tell she wasn't wearing a bra. Dylan tried not to stare, but because of the way she was positioned, one of her breasts was close to spilling out over the top of the tight shirt.

Reaching for the glass, he shook his head to clear away the sensual thoughts the scene in front of him created. He knew that dwelling on the image of her like that would only torment him—especially late at night, alone in his room. That's when he glimpsed something shiny, and a tight knot formed in his stomach.

The chain of her necklace drooped over to one side, and her husband's wedding ring lay nestled in her cleavage. A constant reminder of why they couldn't be together. Why she refused to acknowledge her feelings for him and give the two of them a chance. Dylan wondered if Tessa would ever be able to move on from her life with Ben.

Would she ever allow herself to love *any* other man? Anyone that was—but a Marine. He'd come to resent that symbol of her past. A simple gold band on a simple gold chain. Silly really, it was just a small thing. But it stood in the way of him getting what he wanted. He felt a twinge in the middle of his chest. Was it anger? Was he ashamed to admit he was jealous of an ordinary piece of jewelry?

All of sudden, she stirred under the rumpled sheets and made a sound somewhere between a snore and a snort. Dylan froze. He knew she wasn't going to be happy to see him.

Tessa fought to stay asleep but lost the battle when she felt cool air drift across her face.

"Hey. Sorry, I didn't mean to wake you."

She rubbed her eyes, and slowly his blurry face came into focus. It was Dylan. Inhaling sharply, she blurted, "What are you doing in here?" Instinctively she made an effort to smooth her tangled and matted hair.

When she attempted to sit up, she looked down and discovered how low the front of her shirt was. She immediately reached for the sheet and pulled it up under her chin.

"Don't worry, you didn't have any wardrobe mal-functions why you were sleeping," he said with smirk.

The glaring look on her face along with the color fill-ing her cheeks left no doubt that she didn't find his com-ment, or this situation, the least bit amusing.

"What are you doing in here?" she repeated, irrita-tion clearly evident in her tone. "Where's Mike?"

She'd barely finished her question before she squished up her face and unleashed three booming sneez-es that shook the whole bed.

"He had to leave. Something about a dress Brenda found. I wanted to make sure the air was working in here and that's when I saw your glass was empty," he ex-plained, showing her proof by raising his hand.

He wanted to touch her forehead to see if she had a fever, but decided against it, considering the unpleasant greeting he'd received. He cared about her, but she had made it clear she didn't want anything to do with him. So "Mr. Nice Guy" would have to take a back seat to "Mr. Reality" today. He walked into the bathroom and filled her glass with cold water.

There was a box of cold medicine lying open on the counter, a pencil, and a piece of scratch paper sat next to it with a couple of times scribbled on it. He was puzzled at first until he figured out she must have done that so she wouldn't forget when she'd taken her last dose. He glanced at his watch and tore off one of the perforated squares. "Hold out your hand," he instructed when he made his way back to her.

"Why?" she frowned.

"Because you need to take these before I go heat up some of that soup Mike brought over."

"Maybe I don't want to take any pills right now," she argued, her tone resembling that of a whining child. "And what if I don't want any soup?"

Dylan released a frustrated sigh. "Are you always this difficult when you're sick? Now give me your hand."

"Are you always so bossy?" she shot back.

"It's my nature, besides do you really feel up to arguing with me in your condition?"

Reluctantly, Tessa held up her palm. He pushed two tablets through the thin foil wrapper before handing her the glass of water. He marched toward the door and paused at the end of the bed. "I see you're almost out of tissues. Where do you keep them?"

"Hall closet," she muttered.

Tessa didn't want him here, helping her, taking care of her. Deep down she had to confess it was thoughtful of him to stay, but he wouldn't win any Florence Nightingale award for his bedside manner. She propped herself up against the headboard and waited for him to come back. She was going to strangle Mike the next time she saw him for leaving Dylan here alone with her. *Why did he have to see me looking like death warmed over? Could this day get any worse*? She was positive that the next time she saw him, she'd die from embarrassment.

A few minutes later, he returned with her soup and a new box of tissues. He stayed until she finished eating then put the dirty dishes in the dishwasher. Poking his head in her bedroom, he announced, "I'm leaving now so you can get some beauty sleep." He winked. "It looks like you could use a few hours."

"Is that so?" She flung the almost empty tissue box in his direction, but it didn't even come close to hitting him.

"Nighty night," he taunted.

Tessa could hear him laughing all the way out her front door.

CHAPTER 10

Tessa and Veronica were hard at work in the spacious hotel ballroom, adding and arranging the final touches for the first annual "Hawaii Has Heart" dinner and silent auction.

The event would take place in the same hotel where Veronica had her spa and where her husband, Ruben, was the assistant manager. The money raised would benefit the children's wing at one of the local hospitals.

"The business community really came through with their support, and I know this is going to be an amazing evening." Veronica glanced around the room methodically, pointing here and there with her pen while checking things off the list on the clipboard she was carrying. "I'm so proud of the staff. They certainly out did themselves this time."

"It's wonderful!" Tessa agreed. "I love how people always step up, especially when kids are in need. The quality and quantity of the donations are so much more than we had expected."

Along with a delicious meal and the silent auction, there was going to be a bachelor/bachelorette segment planned where single guests could bid for the opportunity to have dinner with one of the five male or five female participants. At first, the hospital was concerned about the perception something like this would give the charity, but the planning committee assured the board it would be tastefully done. The men would be wearing suits or tuxedos, and the women elegant, and appropriate, evening gowns.

No personal information, other than their names, would be exchanged between the two people before the date. The hotel, which was co-sponsoring the event, had arranged it all. The meals would be served in their dining room and they would be picking up the cost. There would also be a one alcoholic drink maximum.

The charity couldn't afford any bad publicity. If anyone started to get out of hand, security would promptly, but discreetly, handle the situation. The hospital's apprehensions were eased somewhat when two of their own well-respected doctors, one male and one female, agreed to participate.

"I think we're ready," Veronica exhaled, lowering her clipboard.

Tessa nodded as she gazed around the gorgeous ballroom. Sparkling chandeliers hung from the vaulted ceiling casting a warm glow throughout the space. Tables were adorned with candles and fresh flowers, creating an elegant, but welcoming, atmosphere. Her eyes drifted to the decorative clock on the far wall. "Oh my goodness, look at the time! We better hurry and get ready ourselves."

The two women changed in Veronica's spa and some of her employee's did their hair and makeup. They had just finished when Ruben showed up.

He offered them an admiring whistle. "Wow! Look at the two of you!"

His wife gave him a quick peck on the lips. "Hey there, handsome."

"You're both gorgeous, and I'm the lucky man that has the honor of being your escort." He smiled and offered both of his elbows. The two women looped their arms around his and off they went in the direction of the ballroom.

Veronica and Tessa stood on either side of the entrance, greeted the guests, and handed them a program outlining the evening's festivities. Before long, Brenda and Michelle arrived. They congratulated their friends on what a wonderful job they had done and how beautiful they both looked.

"Where's Mike?" Veronica asked, peering over her friend's shoulder.

"He's coming and—we brought another person. I hope you have room," Brenda mentioned rather sheepishly.

"If not, he can have my seat, and I'll sit on his lap," Michelle quickly volunteered, grinning from ear to ear. Her joyful expression faded a little when Brenda elbowed her adding a *don't-even-think-about-it* glare.

Veronica quickly scanned her seating chart and verified that an extra place had been set at their table. "We left a few empty chairs available here and there for last minute additions. But I wish you would have called me." The corners of her mouth lifted slightly, but she still kept her tone all business. She clicked her pen, ready to write down the extra name. "Who is the—"

Just then, Mike and Dylan walked around the corner. Tessa glanced from Brenda to Veronica. The unexpected guest looked very sharp in his black suit. The blue button up shirt complimented the tan in his freshly shaven face and rich-chocolate eyes. The same seductive eyes held a sensual glint as they gave her a once over, from the top of her head, down to her strappy stilettos. She shuddered at the intense assessment. It made her feel vulnerable and exposed. She self-consciously ran a hand down over her stomach and around to her hip to smooth non-existent wrinkles from her gown. His approving smile held a spark of desire as he stared at her.

Dylan studied the image before him. Her strapless dress was a deep plum, the color of the sky at twilight. Fitted at the bust and waist, it flowed down over the rest of her with a slit up one side, exposing a shapely leg.

"You're absolutely breathtaking tonight, Tessa." When he reached for the program she offered him, he captured her hand and rubbed his thumb against the back of her knuckles for barely a moment before she pulled away.

Her breath caught at his touch. He was charming. She'd have to be dead not to notice how sexy he was. Still, she had to get a grip. He sent her senses reeling.

But he was a player, according to Mike. She wasn't interested in a relationship with *any* man right now. She wasn't ready. Especially not with a man who had a reputation for breaking hearts.

And especially not *this* man.

Tessa realized she was still holding her breath and turned away from the rest of them for a few seconds to pull herself together.

"We're all sitting at table twelve." Veronica pointed. "See Ruben over there?"

Dylan reached into his pocket and pulled out a folded check, handing it to Veronica. "Sorry for showing up at the last minute. I wasn't sure about my work schedule and I didn't find out I was able to come until this afternoon."

She grinned and plucked the small piece of paper

from his fingers. "I was hoping you'd be able to attend, so I purposely left room at our table."

The four friends made their way through the crowd and took their seats. Michelle ensured she was sitting next to Dylan, of course. He wished it was Tessa beside him, instead. He'd noticed how intoxicating her perfume was when he had walked past her. Mike was his friend, and he'd asked Dylan not to get involved with Tessa. It appeared Dylan's initial instincts were right. This woman was quickly becoming someone who stirred him and peaked his interest the more he saw her. She wasn't like the other women he'd dated. She was a "relationship" kind of woman. The others were "let's have fun while it lasts" kind of women. Maybe he was ready for a change.

The conversation during dinner was easy and was interspersed with occasional bursts of laughter. The food was delicious and the local bands they'd hired for entertainment were excellent. So far, the evening was a huge success, and the money raised had exceeded everyone's expectations. By the time the servers had cleared most of the dishes, one of the staff hurried over to their table with a frantic look on her face. She whispered something to Veronica that caused her to frown.

"There isn't anyone else who can fill in?" Veronica asked, her voice strained with concern.

All in one breath, words rapidly spilled out from the frazzled employee's mouth, "We asked around and even made a few phone calls, but so far, no one is available."

"All right, let me see what I can do." Veronica rubbed her temples as the young woman scurried away.

Tessa and Brenda leaned in their friend's direction. "What's wrong?"

"One of the men scheduled for the bachelor auction got sick and won't be able make it."

"Can't you just use the four you have left?" Brenda suggested.

The others nodded. That seemed to be the most logical solution.

Veronica paused. "Probably, but the program says five. I'd hate for the charity to appear unorganized or like we're not fulfilling our promises, especially the first year. It will leave a bad impression of the foundation and the hotel. I don't know what I'm going to do."

They stared off into space for a couple of minutes while rhythmically drumming their shiny, painted fingernails on the table. Then Brenda slowly straightened in her chair and beamed. "I've got a great solution."

The other two were eager to hear her revelation.

Brenda motioned with her thumb at the man sitting next to her husband. "How about Dylan?"

The women shifted their focus toward him and they all smiled just as he met their gaze.

"Did I hear my name?"

Brenda reached across her husband and placed her hand on Dylan's arm. "We really need your help."

The looks on his three friends' faces told him he

might regret this. "Oookkaay," he said, drawing out the word. "What's up?"

"One of the men for the bachelor auction had to cancel at the last minute and we need you to fill in for him. Please!" Brenda pleaded.

His jaw fell open. "Excuse me?" He glanced from one hopeful expression to the other, shook his head, and started to chuckle. "No way. Absolutely not!" he declared emphatically.

"Oh come on, Dylan. It's for charity. It's for the hospital," Veronica begged, appealing to his compassionate side.

"Yeah, come on, dude. You think you're such a big stud. Now's the time to prove it," Mike goaded him. "Unless you're chicken and scared you'll embarrass yourself by only raising a few bucks."

Dylan shot his friend a piercing stare. He opened his mouth to tell his buddy what he thought of his comment, but quickly closed his lips tight, realizing the words he wanted to say were not fit for the lovely ladies to hear.

Motioning to Mike to come closer, Dylan whispered so the others couldn't hear, "I'll only do it if Tessa will bid on me," he said, thinking it was a surefire out. He knew Tessa would never go along with it.

Mike considered Dylan's ultimatum then shrugged. "All right.

"Wait!" Dylan grabbed his arm. "So you're okay with this? What about the lecture I got at the barbeque?"

Mike grinned. "It's only a meal together and it's for the kids. I know you'll be a gentleman."

Veronica tapped Dylan on the shoulder to get his attention. "It really would be a big help to me, Dylan if you agreed. It's just one dinner here at the hotel, that's it, nothing more. The proceeds are going to the neo-natal unit at the hospital."

He scowled. *That's fighting dirty, playing the baby card.*

"Will you do it for *me*, Dylan?" Brenda asked.

He had grown to care for her like one of his sisters. He also knew this cause was very near and dear to her heart. Early in their marriage, she and Mike had a baby girl born prematurely who only lived a couple of days. Brenda volunteered, when she could, and always supported the hospitals wherever she was stationed.

Noticing Tessa had been silent this entire time, he turned his attention to her. "What do you think, Ms. Matthews?"

His question caught her off guard. She blushed and fidgeted slightly in her chair. "I think it would be kind and generous of you to help out." She paused. "But the decision is yours."

Dylan studied her for a few seconds. "All right, but only on one condition." The three women leaned closer in anticipation of his demand. "I'll contribute a thousand dollars and Tessa has to use that money to bid on me for the dinner date."

Tessa blinked, inhaled sharply, and sat back in her chair as if she'd been forcefully pushed there. With all eyes focused on her, she scanned the faces at the table. "I—I—but—"

"If she doesn't agree, the deal's off."

Dylan's gaze was intense. Her pulse began to race and heat sizzled on her cheeks. She didn't think this was a good idea, and she didn't appreciate being "the prize" in his plan.

"What if someone out bids that amount?" Veronica, the consummate planner, had to make sure this worked.

"Well then, you five—" He pointed at Mike, Brenda, Tessa, Ruben, and Veronica. "—better pitch in the difference to cover it."

Mike laughed and waved a dismissive hand at his friend. "We don't have anything to worry about. The bid won't go that high for his ugly mug."

"If you weren't married, I'd show you up without even trying," Dylan fired back.

"Wait a minute!" Tessa interrupted the negotiations. "I haven't agreed to this yet!"

Dylan settled back against his chair and crossed his arms over his chest. "Then get yourself another bachelor." He smiled at her, knowing he'd put her in the hot seat. She wasn't going to let her friends down, even it if meant spending a few hours with him.

She knew exactly what he was up to, and she didn't find it amusing.

"You *will* do it, right?" Veronica grabbed her friend's hand and searched her face.

Tessa knew she was stuck and had no choice. She smirked at Dylan. "Sure, after all it's for charity. How bad could one dinner be?"

Making a face, he pretended he'd been wounded by her response. "I can guarantee you won't be disappointed." He arched his eyebrows for emphasis, partly because he wanted to watch her squirm, just a little.

Her coy grin vanished as his words sank in, sending thoughts and images flooding her mind. Danger alarms screamed in her head and her heart pounded like a jackhammer. She was treading in dangerous waters. A rogue shark was on the loose and hunting for his next victim. She had to guard her heart vigorously from being ripped apart by his razor-sharp charm, slick smooth talk, and deadly good looks.

"Thank you so much, Dylan!" Rising from her chair, Veronica tugged on his arm, "Let's get you to the back and make sure you're all ready to go."

All of sudden it hit him. *What have I gotten myself into just so I can spend a little time with Tessa?*

Michelle had been mingling around the room and returned to the table just as the two were walking away. "Where are they going?"

After Brenda explained the whole story, Michelle grabbed Tessa's arm. "I wanna bid on him! Can we share?"

All eyes centered on her and, as if they had rehearsed it, Mike, Brenda, and Tessa chimed together, "No!"

"I don't know why I hang around you guys. You never want me to have a good time." Straightening her spine, she lifted her chin. "Fine, I'll go buy one of my own." After she stormed off, the friends discussed whether they should warn Veronica and the other bachelors, but they all decided against it.

Ruben offered his opinion of the situation. "Let Michelle have her fun, it's only dinner. Beside how bad could it be?"

The rest looked at each and then burst out laughing. He didn't know her as well as her friends did, obviously. But they *did* know her.

"What?" Ruben asked innocently.

"Look," Mike started. "She's a good kid and basically harmless but she can get...how can I put this?...over-the-top sometimes around good-looking guys."

"You mean like stalking them sexually, or what?" Ruben frowned. "Do I need to call security?"

"No," Brenda chimed in. "She's a nice person. She'd never do anything *really* bad. She only likes to flirt and hug and stuff like that." She chuckled. "You know what's funny? If she really *does* like a guy, she gets all quiet and almost shy around him. We all love her, she's just Michelle."

Ruben looked confused, but didn't ask any more questions.

Dylan was the last man to walk out, and he was feeling more anxious by the minute. He loved getting attention from a woman, but this was different. He'd heard stories from friends of his that had worked bridal bachelorette parties, and some of those females were flat out crazy. *But this is a* classy *event, right? Yeah, but this is* still *a mistake.*

"Get ready, you're next." Veronica touched his arm before she disappeared through the heavy black curtain.

"All right, ladies. We have a substitution from your program." Groans and rumblings stirred through the crowd. "Wait, wait," she shouted, finally gaining their attention. "You won't be disappointed, trust me. The next bachelor may be last, but he's definitely not least. Please put your hands together and welcome, Gunnery Sergeant Dylan Cooper," she announced with flare and excitement.

He came out from behind the curtain and immediately long eyelashes batted in his direction. Winks and seductive smiles were also aimed in his direction. A few excited giggles and appreciative oohs and ahhs spread throughout the group of eager females. He walked tentatively down the elevated stage, looking nervously to the right, then to the left. At the end of the runway, he stiffly turned around then, like Veronica had told him to, and walked back to the curtain.

She caught his arm and whispered in his ear. "Loosen up, have fun with it. Remember what Mike said."

That smug look and challenge his friend had given

him triggered something in Dylan. He spotted his buddy at the table and Mike was pointing and laughing. *Okay, II'll show him.*

Dylan also saw Tessa and thought about how much he wanted to go on this date with her. So he decided he might as well go for it. This time, he strutted down the runway and struck a pose as if he had been modeling for years. He started to grin, nod, and point at all the pretty women throughout the room. He focused on Tessa again, winked, and added a subtle swivel of his hips. The group of ladies went wild.

Veronica urged the women to start spending their money. "What do I hear as an opening bid for dinner with Sergeant Cooper?"

"One hundred," a voice called from the back of the room.

"One hundred and fifty," another female shouted from somewhere off to the right of the stage.

"Two hundred." Tessa spoke up, trying to sound enthusiastic. *How ridiculous. I can't believe I got talked into doing something like this.* If it weren't for the kids, she never would have agreed. Plus, it wasn't her money.

The bidding continued with enthusiastic women, young and old, clambering for a date with the sexy Marine. The higher the bids went, the more Dylan poured on the charm. He'd unbutton his suit jacket and shove his hands into the front pockets of his pants—or place them on his hips. With one leg slightly forward, he pivoted and spun around slowly a time or two as if he were a seasoned male model on a runway in New York. He continued to smile politely at each female, but always returned his attention to Tessa. The bidding was slowing down and she thought she'd teach him a lesson. It was going to cost him to have dinner with her. The last bid had been six hundred and fifty.

"Eight hundred," she shouted confidently and saw Dylan's jaw twitch slightly.

He knew what she was up to, and he had to laugh a little at himself. It served him right. She was a tough cookie. Murmurs spread the crowd then they quieted, waiting to see if anyone would bid higher. Tessa sent Veronica a look, encouraging her to hurry up and end this charade.

"Going, going…"

"Fifteen hundred dollars," a velvet voice from the back of the room slowly offered.

Gasps could be heard, followed by low whispers rippling through the ladies standing around the stage as they parted, making a center aisle. A tall, auburn-haired woman appeared, gliding forward through the crowd. Her designer, emerald gown hugged a voluptuous *Playboy* centerfold figure. She gazed up at Dylan, who looked like a deer caught in headlights. He jerked his head up, looking for Mike, silently reminding him of the deal they had all made. His friend just shrugged.

Tessa knew she better think of something fast. She

didn't want Dylan to be mad at Veronica, thinking they had all backed out on the deal. "Sixteen hundred dollars," she managed, not nearly as triumphant as her previous bid. She made her way forward and once again glared at Veronica to hurry and end this. The two women were alone in the center of the room.

"Marvelous! Okay, going, going..."

"Two—thousand—dollars," the sultry beauty drawled, taking one step closer to the runway—and her prize.

Dylan knew his fate was sealed. His friends couldn't come up with an extra thousand, and he didn't expect them to. It had been sweet of Tessa to try, and he would have helped his friends pitch in the other six hundred somehow, but now that point was moot.

Veronica banged the gavel. "Going, going, gone. Congratulations to the lady in green."

Dylan stepped off the stage and the lovely woman waiting for him introduced herself.

"My name is Sable. I'm looking forward to our evening together." She pulled a business card from her cocktail clutch and tucked it into the breast pocket of his suit coat. Patting it gently, she let her hand linger there and stared deep into his eyes. "Here's my number so we can arrange the date."

He glanced down to where her palm rested and wondered if she could feel his heart pounding through the material. He met her intense gaze before answering.

"Actually, our dinner will be coordinated through the hotel."

The corners of her bright red lips eased upward as a sensual playfulness twinkled in dark green eyes that matched her dress. Gently placing a hand on his shoulder, she encouraged him forward.

Her warm breath tickled his neck as she whispered seductively in his ear, "Give me a call, Sergeant Cooper. I promise it will be a night you'll *never* forget."

Her silky hair brushed his cheek and he inhaled her exotic perfume.

A cool shiver skittered down his spine. She moved away from him, but before he could say anything, she sashayed out of the room, leaving him standing there— stunned and intrigued.

An odd sensation shot through Tessa as she watched this mysterious woman touch, Dylan, whisper in his ear, and smile at him.

Michelle walked up and stood next to her. "That's too bad. You won't be having a date with Mr. Sexy."

"Um, huh," Tessa mumbled.

"Are you okay?"

"Why wouldn't I be?"

Michelle shook her head. "If I didn't know better, I'd say that expression on your face resembles the color of her dress."

"What?"

"You're jealous of her. After all you're fussing and

fuming, you were looking forward to having dinner with him, weren't you?"

Tessa scowled. "Be serious! I was just going along with the plan for Veronica and the charity."

"Yeah, okay. And I've got some great ocean front property just outside Death Valley for sale." Michelle laughed and wandered off to search for some of the single men that didn't win a date with any of the bachelorettes. Tessa thought about what her friend had said. Those same sensations tugged at her again. The ones she'd experienced when she'd first seen him tonight. *It couldn't be that, could it? Why do I care if he goes to dinner with that gorgeous woman? Jealous? Me? No way! That would mean I'm interested in him.*

And I'm not.

Am I?

CHAPTER 11

Saturday night, Tessa drove over to Brenda's house to help her get ready for the Marine Corps Ball. They carefully pinned soft curls on top of her head. A few wispy tendrils framed Brenda's face and kissed the back of her neck. A long, silky, red dress fit her body as if it had been designed just for her.

"I wish you were going tonight. We'd have so much fun," Brenda called from her walk-in closet.

"I'm actually looking forward to a quiet night at home. Playing dress up is more your thing, anyway," Tessa teased.

Dangling red stilettos from her fingertips, Brenda walked across the room. "You gonna be okay seeing Dylan when he comes over?"

"Of course. Why wouldn't I?"

The closer it got to his arrival, the more butterflies showed up, uninvited, to party in Tessa's stomach.

"Don't try to fool me." Brenda wagged an index finger at her. "You may want to deny it, but I know you like him more than you are willing to admit."

Tessa waved her off with a dismissive sound, like air escaping a tire. "I don't know what you're talking about."

Turning away from her friend, Tessa busied herself trying to locate just the right shade of lipstick. She knew the expression on her face would expose her as a liar. She needed to prepare herself mentally to see the man that sent her heart rate soaring every time he was near her.

Brenda wasn't deterred. "I've seen the way you look at him when you don't think anyone is watching. I know you wanted to win that date with him at the auction. You deserve to be happy. Maybe it's time you allow yourself to love again."

Scrambling for a way out of this uncomfortable topic of conversation, Tessa forced a grin. "I'm sure he had a wonderful time with Ms. Emerald Dress. Besides, tonight isn't about me, it's about you."

"Okay, but I know I'm right. I should probably tell you—" Brenda paused, her voice less playful. "Dylan's bringing a date."

Tessa recalled the day when he had asked her to the ball at the sports bar after the football game. She'd almost agreed. A rush of emotions squeezed around her heart like tentacles. Thankfully, he hadn't told Mike, or Brenda would know. And she would have never heard the end of it. "Good for him."

Brenda planted her hands on her hips. "Is that all you have to say?"

"I'd have been shocked if he *wasn't* bringing one."

"Fine." Brenda sighed, clearly frustrated. "Pretending you don't care doesn't change the fact that it's true."

Tessa looked around the room and smiled. It was a perfect mixture of Mike and Brenda. Masculine and feminine. Various pictures from his years in the Marines hung next to vacation photos of them together. A few flowery oil paintings added touches of color to offset some of Mike's things in the drab olive green used by the military. His boots lay on the carpet next to her high heels, his cammies and uniforms hung alongside her designer dresses.

"What are you smiling about?" Brenda asked. "You had a faraway look in your eyes."

Tessa shook her head. "Nothing really. Just how normal this room looks to us, but how strange it would seem to a civilian."

Brenda looked puzzled. "What do you mean?"

"Look over there on your dresser. You have three or four very expensive bottles of perfume sitting next to one of Mike's aircraft training manuals."

"It's just so natural to me. I don't pay attention anymore."

"I remember when Ben and I first got married. I thought all the terminology was so weird." Her friend nodded in agreement as Tessa continued. "Hats are called covers, and four day weekends are called 96s. Oh, but the craziest one I remember is the little tie tack thing on the back of the medals and bars are called turtles."

Both women laughed at that one. Tessa appreciated sharing a lighter moment, considering that later in the day things might be more difficult.

They soon returned their attention back to the last few details of selecting just the right earrings and necklace to complete Brenda's outfit. Minimal make-up accentuated her flawless skin. Smokey eye shadow along with red lipstick made her look as if she were about to walk down a crimson carpet at her latest movie premier.

Tessa smiled. "Girl, you look gorgeous. New-York-fashion-week gorgeous."

Brenda studied her reflection in the floor length mirror in the master bathroom and chuckled. "Thanks. You're so good for my ego. No wonder I love having you for my friend." She added a few dabs of her favorite Prada perfume to her wrists and throat.

Following Brenda out of the bedroom, Tessa stood quietly in the background. She noticed how Mike watched in awe as his wife descended the stairs, step by step.

He greeted her with a wide-eyed look of amazement, a sparkle in his eyes, and a long, low whistle.

When she reached her husband, Brenda rewarded him with a playful curtsy. "Well, thank you, kind sir."

"Wow, you look stunning, sweetheart. You're even more beautiful than the day we got married. And I didn't think that was possible."

Color invaded Brenda's cheeks before he wrapped her in a long hug.

"You clean up pretty good yourself, Mike," Tessa chimed in.

He grunted. "Gee, thanks."

These two people were very special to her. Tessa loved watching them display such tender affection for one another. Still, sadness gripped her heart, knowing she'd felt that way once, too—and at the very real possibility she would never experience that feeling again.

Brenda beamed up at her husband with her palms resting against his chest. "You look so dashing in your dress blues. Every time you wear them, I fall in love with you all over."

He placed a soft kiss on her cheek then leaned over and breathed something in her ear that Tessa couldn't hear. Whatever it was, it made Brenda giggle and blush again.

"Okay, you love birds, save all the mushy stuff for *after* the ball," Tessa teased.

Just then, there was a knock on the front door—Dylan had arrived.

When Mike invited him in, Tessa thought she was

going to faint. That could happen to a woman when you took an already good-looking man and put him in a Marine dress blue uniform. However, her reaction hadn't been this strong since the last time she'd seen Ben wearing his.

Dylan stood in the entryway along with his date. She was breathtakingly beautiful. Her coal black hair hung in long, loose curls down her back and, with her tanned skin, she had an exotic appearance. The pale-pink gown she wore clung to a body that belonged on the cover of a Victoria Secret magazine.

After greeting Mike and Brenda, he turned to his left and smiled. "Hey, Tessa."

Cold shivers raced down her spine. "Hi." Her voice squeaked. The rush of jealousy that welled up inside her when he placed his palm on the small of the other woman's back took Tessa by surprise.

"Everyone, this is Gabriella."

The other three greeted her with a friendly "Hello," or "Nice to meet you."

Mike raised his eyebrows and shot his friend a look of male approval.

"You're lovely in that dress," the newcomer said, motioning toward Brenda.

Dylan was quick to agree.

"Thank you. And that's the perfect shade of pink on you," Brenda said.

Smoothing her hands over front of her gown, Gabriella smiled. "Thanks. Your husband looks sharp tonight, too."

Dylan cleared his throat. "Yeah, this uniform can even make a homely mutt like him look *pretty*."

Everyone laughed at Mike's expense.

While the women talked, Dylan glanced over at Tessa again. A longing tugged at his heart. He suddenly wished she had accepted his invitation and she was the one going with him instead. It didn't matter that she was wearing an old T-shirt, jeans, and tennis shoes. The elegantly dressed female standing next to him couldn't compete with how Tessa made him feel.

After the five of them engaged in polite conversation for a few minutes, Brenda looked down at her watch. "It's about that time. We better get going."

"Are you *sure* you're gonna be okay?" Brenda whispered in her friend's ear.

"I'll be fine," Tessa reassured her as she fought to hide her true feelings. "Don't worry about me. Go and have fun with your cute husband.

Brenda grinned as she peeked over her shoulder. "He does look yummy, doesn't he?"

Following the two couples outside, Tessa took some pictures and gave Brenda one last hug. "Have a good time everyone," she said, waving good-bye, and watched them drive away.

Leaving her behind—and alone.

Tessa's ride home, though short in distance, felt as if

it took hours instead of minutes. It was unsettling. She could feel her emotions boiling up dangerously close to the surface. By the time she arrived and was safe inside her house with the doors locked, tears had turned her bottom lashes into tiny black spikes of mascara. A boulder sized lump burned in her throat, making swallowing more difficult with every passing second.

Distraction. Yeah, that's what I need, a distraction. Plopping down on the couch, she picked up a magazine and started paging through it. She soon realized she couldn't concentrate on the pictures, let alone read any of the articles. *Noise. Maybe noise will help.* Clicking on the TV, Tessa flipped through the channels, but nothing held her attention. Finally, she gave up and shut off the infomercial that tried to convince her she couldn't live without their new-fangled vegetable chopper. Crazy thoughts forced their way into her mind, and although she knew better, she couldn't stop herself.

Walking into her bedroom closet, she retrieved a garment bag, hidden way in the back behind winter coats she hadn't used since moving to Hawaii. After laying it on the bed, she stared at it for a minute or two. Tessa wrestled with the idea of whether or not she could actually deal with what she would find inside. Her trembling fingers tentatively lowered the zipper. Next, she carefully slid the protective covering off the top edges of the garment to expose a familiar jacket.

She brushed her fingertips lightly over the dark blue

fabric and the shiny gold buttons. Memories of the wonderful man who had once worn this uniform drifted in from her past. Heartache clouded her vision. She guided her index finger slowly over the rows of medals and colorful bars that adorned the regal coat. She remembered how handsome he'd looked in it the day they were married and at the last ball they had attended a few short months before he deployed.

Hot, pain-filled tears stung her eyes, again. The droplets landed on the cherished reminder of happier times.

Gathering up the uniform, still in the bag, she hugged it to her chest, and cried for several minutes. She prayed with all of her heart that her late husband's arms would magically fill the sleeves. She longed for him to hold her close one more time while she struggled through this latest battle with loneliness.

But he didn't.

After drying her tears, she tenderly caressed the jacket again, straightened the material, and zipped the bag closed. She returned the treasured memory to the far back corner of her closet.

Curling up on her bed, Tessa gazed through her window as dusk painted the tropical sky vibrant shades of yellows and oranges against a dark lavender canvas. She was tired of crying over what she had lost—and what could've been.

"I miss you so much, Ben. But I can't keep living like this. I know you wouldn't want me to continually dwell in the past," she whispered, holding tight to the ring around her neck. "Everyone tells me you'd want me to live my life and move on. I know they're right. I'm just so scared." When she spoke those words, something sparked inside her. People said those same words to her over and over. Yet somehow today, hearing her own voice say them out loud, it was different. She was finally giving herself permission to be happy, to start over. Even though it wouldn't be easy, she *knew* she had to try.

The image of how Dylan looked this evening suddenly appeared in her thoughts. He could be the national poster boy for tall, dark, and handsome. Her stomach muscles quivered, recalling how sexy he had looked in his dress blues.

The crisp white cover sat atop his recently trimmed high-and-tight as if it were a royal crown fit for a king. The seams along the top of the jacket strained slightly against his muscular shoulders. His chest tapered down to a narrow waist encircled with a white belt. Royal blue pants were accented with a scarlet strip of fabric sewn on the outside of each leg, starting at the waist and ending at the hem. They formed the illusion that his legs were even longer than they actually were. His black dress shoes shined with a high gloss, like polished onyx.

She wasn't sure why, but seeing Dylan earlier this evening had forced her to face the fact that she *had* developed feelings for him. The man she had fought so hard to push away. *But what about him? He seems interested.*

She thought she'd seen a glimpse of something in his eyes when he looked at her, a look somewhere between lust and genuine affection. *It must've just been my imagination.* She shook her head. Yet her heart insisted this time was different somehow.

There was one thing that Tessa *was* sure about.

She knew she had to give him a chance.

It was time.

ᏮᎧᏮᎧ

After arriving at the ball, Dylan was in no mood for a celebration. He couldn't stop thinking about Tessa. Gabriella noticed how distant and quiet he was, and she asked him if everything was all right.

He knew he shouldn't have to try so hard to enjoy her company. "I'm fine. I just have a lot on my mind." He forced a smile at the beautiful woman sitting next to him. "Would you like to dance?"

She nodded and gracefully rose from her chair. "I'd love to."

The entire time he held her in his arms, he wished it was Tessa pressed against him, *her* warm breath on his neck, *her* perfume filling his nostrils. He'd be willing to bet that almost every man in the room would kill to trade places with him right now. And yet, he was daydreaming about a woman he couldn't have.

Later, Mike caught up with him. "Hey, what's up

with you tonight? You're acting as if you're here with a warthog in a dress."

"I'm just preoccupied, you know, work's been crazy—"

"Don't give me that line of crap. What's really going on?" Mike pressed.

He wasn't quite sure how his friend would react to what he was about to tell him. "I wish Tessa were here."

"I see. So you didn't listen to what I said at my house that night?"

"Nope." Dylan paused. "She's…There's just something…"

"I know. I witnessed the sparks between you two at the auction." Mike stared at Dylan for a moment. "You care about her? I mean more than the other women you usually date?"

Dylan nodded, feeling as if he'd been called to the principal's office. "I'm afraid so."

Mike placed his hand firmly on his friend's shoulder. "If you're being straight with me, then why not tell her?"

"Because she's made it perfectly clear that she doesn't want anything to do with me or any other Marine."

"She's just scared. And I can't say as I blame her. Tell her how you feel, and then take it slow. You'll never know unless you try."

Dylan arched his eyebrows. "So, *now* I have your blessing?"

"I've thought about it, and I've had my doubts that you could stop chasing the ladies. So as long as you're sure about this, I can't think of anyone I'd rather see her end up with." Mike stuck out his hand and shook Dylan's. "Now, don't get me wrong, I love Tessa like family but damn, son, you've got it bad, don't you? Especially if you're ignoring a knockout like Gabriella," Mike added with a chuckle to lighten the mood. "Now quit your whining and buy me a beer."

As the two men headed for the bar, Dylan felt relieved, as if a weight had been lifted off of him. Not that he *needed* Mike's approval, but he did appreciate his friendship and support.

There was only one thing left to do.

Convince Tessa he was the man for her.

CHAPTER 12

Dylan got a major surprise when he called Tessa and asked her, again, to go out with him. She agreed! Things were looking up.

Friday night, he and Tessa drove up to Paradise Cove to enjoy a luau. She had been looking forward to watching the dancers and hearing the stories of the different cultures featured in the performances. Mike and Brenda were originally supposed to have joined them, but something came up at the last minute, and they had to cancel.

She and Dylan had been to a couple of dinners at Mike and Brenda's house to ease her slowly back into this "dating" process. Tessa had explained to Dylan that she didn't want to rush into anything, and he said he understood. She was nervous how her heart would react and the possibility of her bolting if things became too intense, too quickly. Every time she was near him, electricity surged through her veins.

And that scared the hell out of her.

But she had made a decision. It was time to take a deep breath, pull on her big-girl panties, and see where this relationship might lead.

The parking lot had started to fill up with tour buses by the time Dylan and Tessa arrived. He dropped her off near the entrance so she could wait in line while he found a spot for his truck. When he finally joined her, she introduced him to a group of three older ladies from Ireland. Tessa had been talking with them about what other sites they should see while visiting Oahu. She chuckled when she saw their eyes brighten the minute Dylan arrived. The Irish ladies began flirting with him, touching his arm, and letting their hands linger there awhile. They even giggled like teenagers when he flirted back, tossing a sexy smile or two in their direction.

A few minutes before the gates opened, a couple of employees strolled among the waiting guests handing out traditional leis. A fragrant aroma engulfed them. The purple, yellow, and white colors of the flowers were deep and vivid. Some of the men received beaded leis made from black or dark brown kukui nuts. Once they were allowed inside, Dylan and Tessa followed the path that wound through a grove of tall palm trees. On each side of the walkway, various species of green plants covered the ground, making them feel as if they were in the heart of a tropical jungle. Off to the left, a woman wearing a colorful native dress sang softly as she stood inside a gazebo with a thatched, umbrella shaped roof.

At the end walkway, before entering the lush grounds and entertainment area, they had their picture taken with two of the dancers performing tonight.

Several rows of festively decorated tables were arranged on the sand. Dylan's fingers gently cupped Tessa's elbow. "Where would you like to sit?"

"Near the stage if possible. Is that all right with you?"

He winked. "That works for me. Hey, the closer to those swaying hips, the better."

His expression evoked two images in her mind: one of a two-year-old little boy eyeing an ice cream cone and the other of a thirteen-year-old boy anxiously opening the cover of his first dirty magazine. "Am I going to have to order you a drool bib?" she teased.

"Oh, like you aren't going to be doing the same thing when you see those young, shirtless guys with rock hard abs."

Tessa didn't answer him, but he saw her cheeks turn a rosy pink.

The tables filled up quickly and they introduced themselves to the people around them. Sitting next to Tessa was an older couple.

"Hi, we're Dave and Bonnie," the man said. "We're

visiting from Denver to celebrate our fortieth wedding anniversary."

Tessa smiled. "Congratulations."

Bonnie gazed lovingly at her husband for a few seconds before turning to face the others. "We met here in Hawaii when he was in the Navy and I was a nurse. We were married before he was transferred back to the states."

Next to Dylan, was a young couple who looked barely old enough to vote. The guy spoke next. "I'm Jeff and this here's Candi. We're from Chicago."

Candi's summery dress didn't leave much to the imagination. Spaghetti straps strained atop her shoulders trying to support the weight of her ample chest, allowing a good amount of cleavage to show. "That's Candi with an 'I,'" she said in a high-pitched giggle. "We just got married yesterday on the beach." With her eyes huge, she placed a hand over her heart, "It was sooo roomaantic," she added, drawing out each syllable.

Tessa wasn't sure she liked being surrounded by all this love—especially sitting so close to Dylan.

A few minutes later, they excused themselves and took a walk around. Immaculately manicured lawns edged with neatly trimmed hedges and more palm trees created the perfect atmosphere.

The grass felt spongy under foot, like nothing Tessa had ever walked on before.

She pointed at a spot behind the stage. "Oh look!"

Two, small, brown animals that resembled large, ground squirrels scurried about. "Aren't they cute?"

Dylan didn't seem too impressed but nodded anyway.

When an employee walked by, Tessa stopped him and motioned in the direction of the frolicking creatures. "Excuse me, what are those?"

"Mongoose, ma'am," he told her, before continuing on his way.

Dylan and Tessa strolled past the hedges over to a low, rock wall backed by more green plants. Below was a small embankment that lead to a rocky shoreline and then to the deep blue ocean. Several people were taking pictures, wanting to capture memories of a dream vacation. Tessa offered to help the other guests so everyone in their group could be in the photo. Someone volunteered to return the favor, and Dylan readily accepted. Leaning his back on a nearby palm tree, he wrapped his arms around Tessa's waist and hugged her close. He could feel her tense, but she didn't try to move away.

Her nerves sparked as her spine rested against his firm chest. She slid her arms under his. She didn't want him to discover how badly her stomach was quivering. To make things worse, right before the man snapped their picture, Dylan lowered head and, in a deep and seductive tone, only loud enough for her to hear, he whispered, "Smile pretty for the camera."

Tessa apologized and politely asked the man to take

the shot again. As a result of his raspy voice breathing so close to her ear, she was positive there had been a strange look on her face. Somewhere between shock and terror, she guessed.

Finally, it was time to take the pig out of the pit. The staff invited the guests to sit on bleachers or stand nearby while a brightly dressed employee described what was happening. Two bare-chested men with traditional garments wrapped around their waists walked over to a cement slab with the middle of it covered in leaves. They pulled back the outer layers until they reached the prize buried underneath. Wrapped in a mesh, was half a pig, roasted to perfection. They removed it from the pit and placed it on a large, flat tray with wooden handles on either side.

One man grabbed the two front handles, the other the two back handles, and they carried it past the crowd. The meal was served shortly after that. There was quite a variety on the plate: pork, chicken, fish, green beans, white rice, and of course, poi.

"The food's delicious," Tessa said after sampling a little bit of everything.

Wrinkling up her nose, Candi pointed. "What's this purple, gooey stuff?"

"That's poi," Bonnie replied. "It a traditional Hawaiian staple made from the taro root. Try it."

The young woman dipped her finger into the thick substance. "Yuck, it tastes like paste."

"It's not that bad," Dylan said. "It just takes a little getting used to." His comment was met with another cringe of disgust.

Some of the performers danced while the guests enjoyed their food, and the emcee talked about the various cultures. She involved the crowd by having them repeat that *mahalo* means thank you and *aloha* means hello *and* goodbye.

The three couples ate and talked during the rest of dinner. About the time everyone had finished eating, several people wandered over to the grassy area next to the stage. Tessa realized the daylight was beginning to fade. "I'd love to get a good sunset photo. Do you mind?"

"Let's go." Dylan was more than willing to spend time with her in the shadowy moonlight.

They joined the others near the rock wall to watch the sky change from a calm robin's egg blue into a scenic post card. Soon, a vivid brush stroke of orange lay next to the water on the horizon. It slowly faded up to yellow in places and then to a smoky purple as it kissed the evening sky.

"I never get tired of watching how magnificently day turns into night here in Hawaii," she sighed.

"It is amazing," he agreed.

She snapped a few pictures, then they just stood quietly, enjoying the last few moments of the magical transformation as the sun disappeared below the horizon.

When she turned to head back to their table, Dylan

gently laid his hand on the side of her neck, allowing his thumb to caress her cheek. "You're so beautiful, Tessa. I shouldn't have waited so long tonight to tell you."

She glanced down at the ground, focusing her eyes on the patch of grass between their feet. The compliment made her feel uneasy and, yet, stirred exhilarating sensations in her that she hadn't expected. "We—" she started, but wasn't allowed to finish.

His hand slid around the back of her neck and tilted her head so he could gaze into her eyes. "But I *can't* wait any longer for this."

As his lips met hers, Tessa protested, but only for a second. Soon all the reasons they shouldn't were incinerated into ashes by the fire his kiss had ignited inside of her. The ground suddenly felt like it was giving way under her feet, as if she was sinking. Something was wrong. She grabbed for his shirt and slid her hands up around his neck. Her legs buckled, unable to support her, as if the bones had been removed. Using his right arm, Dylan tightened his embrace around her back to prevent her from landing in a puddle of embarrassing female hormones at his feet. The fingers of his left hand skillfully teased the golden strands at the nape of her neck. Tingles spread like wild fire across her sensitive skin. His kisses made her dizzy. Her head spun in circles. Finally, she broke away from him to catch her breath.

Dylan's heart was pounding and his breathing was shallow. Why did it have to be *her* that he wanted? A woman who'd made it clear she didn't want a *serious* relationship with someone like him? Was that it? For the challenge? The idea that he had to get what he was told he couldn't have? Maybe at first, but not now. Tessa was more than just another conquest. He could have his pick of beautiful women that would date him willingly. So why was he trying so hard to win over the one that refused to give him a *real* chance? Male pride?

Whatever it was, Tessa Matthews had him all tied up in knots and feeling things he hadn't felt before. He probably should be more cautious, especially since she'd been emphatic that they needed to take things slow. She wanted to be friends, for now. He smiled. *She sure didn't kiss me like a friend.* Dylan liked the obvious effect their kissing had on her. She felt good in his arms. It felt right. He couldn't remember a time when he'd experienced a more powerful first kiss with a woman.

Tessa hadn't been prepared for how their few fleeting moments of intimacy had jolted her body with electricity and pleasure that she hadn't experienced in quite some time. She couldn't think. A part of her wanted to be back in his arms, and another part chastised her for allowing him to make her feel so vulnerable. Things were moving way too fast and getting way too real. She didn't get the impression he was acting like a playboy. There was a caring and an honesty about him in the way he looked at her tonight. His feelings for her seemed genuine.

And that scared her most of all.

Both were quiet after they returned to the table, and the older couple seemed to notice. Dave winked at Dylan, adding a chuckle. "We thought maybe you two got lost out there in the moonlight."

Tessa felt color tint her cheeks.

"Now, honey, don't embarrass them," Bonnie scolded. "It wasn't that long ago that we used to go for long walks under the stars, and you'd steal a smooch or two."

Dylan saw Tessa's blush deepened a shade. He hadn't meant to make her uncomfortable, but he didn't regret the kiss. Hoping to draw attention away from Tessa, he reached across the table and clinked glasses with the older man, sort of a modified high five.

"I hope we're still in love as much as you guys when we're *your* age," the barely twenty-something, bride chimed in.

"Don't worry about it, babe. I'll still think you're hot," her cherub-faced husband assured her. "Especially if you're still rockin' this killer bikini bod."

He grabbed her around the waist and tickled her. When she released a high-pitched squeal, he silenced her with an overly amorous kiss. The other four exchanged knowing glances that held the wisdom of experience before shaking their heads and moving on to other topics of conversation.

Soon, more dancers filled the stage, accompanied by drums and other instruments. For each song, the costumes changed slightly. The males had a cloth or tan grass skirt draped over shorts and headbands made of feathers, leaves, or beads. The bronzed, shirtless men would flex their arm, stomach, and leg muscles, then stomp, shout, or yell during the song. Sometimes they would pound the stage with narrow wooden poles as tall as they were.

The females wore a larger variety of outfits, from coconuts bras and large feathered headpieces to long dresses similar to those worn by Native Americans. The tanned, hourglass lower bodies of the exotic-looking women would shake and shimmy while their upper bodies barely moved. Tessa was amazed at how fast they could wiggle their hips. More than once she caught a few of them glancing Dylan's way. They smiled and batted their eyelashes when they didn't think anyone would notice how their eyes lingered on him more than some of the other men.

He stared intently as the women performed. "Careful, your inner cave man is showing," Tessa mocked and playfully lifted his napkin to the corner of his mouth.

He snatched the cloth from her hand. "Very funny." A second later, he refocused his attention on the stage.

"Hey, guys, too bad we forgot our grass clippers tonight," Dave bellowed, and Dylan heartily agreed.

Jeff, however, looked confused. "I'm pretty sure this place has a person they pay to do that stuff. Besides, why are you guys thinking about cutting grass with these Hawaiian hotties struttin' their stuff right in front of you?"

Dylan and Dave looked at each other and then back to the young man before they started to explain, but Bonnie stopped them. "Never mind, Jeff. These two were just trying to be funny."

The newlyweds just shrugged.

Tessa's favorite dance was the traditional hula. A woman slowly swayed her hips and, at the same time, her hands would gracefully tell an ancient story of her ancestors. There was also a man who twirled baton-type sticks that were on fire at both ends. Next, a couple dressed in all white performed the Hawaiian wedding song. It was lovely and very romantic.

Tessa noticed the older couple gazing tenderly at each other and, when the dance was over, Bonnie dabbed her eyes.

Tessa leaned over. "Are you okay?"

"Oh, I'm fine. We had that at our ceremony, so it means a lot to us," the older woman explained.

Tessa nodded. "I'm sure your day was beautiful."

Bonnie beamed. "It was."

A few minutes later, the emcee announced that the dancers would be coming out among the guests in search of volunteers to bring up on stage to learn the hula.

One of the very beautiful women, that had caught Dylan's attention, walked right up to him and grabbed his hand. "Come on, sugar. I'm gonna teach you to shake those hips."

She demonstrated her talents for him, up close and

personal. Before she even finished her sentence, he was out of his chair, as excited as a kid who'd just been offered a ride in a spaceship.

All the volunteers lined up on the platform and received a quick lesson before the music began. The crowd roared with laughter. First on stage was an overweight man in sandals, socks, sunburned, bald head, and a size too small Hawaiian shirt. He was soon joined by a woman who looked like Aunt Bea, Candi, five or six others, and a few kids. And Dylan rounded out the group.

Tessa joined the rest of the guests in cheering them on. She covered her mouth as she burst out laughing while watching the bald man and the older lady. They were hysterical.

"Shake it, baby! Yeah, woo hoo! That's my girl!" Jeff called out right before he let go an ear-piercing wolf whistle.

Then Tessa's eyes fell on Dylan. He was laughing and having a good time. He could sway his hips with the best of them. She would have never thought a man built like him could move like that. He caught her staring at him and added an extra bump and grind just for her. Her amusement suddenly faded, heat returned to her cheeks, and the spark inside her flared up again. Why did he have such a potent effect on her? She hadn't known him that long. Yet, he could make her heart leap in her chest with only a smile.

Dylan and Candi rejoined the others, but immediately he could sense something was different about Tessa. "Are you okay?"

She nodded. "I'm fine, just a little tired."

He'd been around women long enough to take an educated guess that was actually code for, "I don't want to talk about it."

The three couples chatted a while more, and then it was time to leave. The newlyweds both had a little too much to drink, and Dylan was relieved to find out they were part of a tour group, so neither would be driving tonight.

Just as he was relaying that information to Dave, Candi took off for the shadows. "Catch me if you can," she squealed over her shoulder.

Jeff stumbled in the soft sand, chasing after her. "You owe me a kiss when I do."

The others heard Candi's high-pitch giggle, and then her tone changed. "Oh no, one of my straps broke," she announced slightly annoyed. "This is a brand new dress."

"Here, babe, I'll help," her husband volunteered.

A heavy sigh cooed from the darkness. "Jeffy, that's not my strap."

"I know," he growled seductively.

"I wonder if the management knows there's another kind of show getting started out there in the bushes," Dave announced with a big smile.

"Yeah, an X-rated one. I'd say Candi with an 'I' is about to get a lot more than just a kiss," Dylan added. "I don't know why she's surprised her outfit had a structural problem. After all, she was asking an awful lot from those two tiny pieces of string."

The two men laughed, and the women rolled their eyes, slapping each man on the arm.

A few minutes went by and Dave thought he better interrupt the two lovebirds. He made sure his voice was loud enough for them to hear.

"Maybe you two better get going. You don't want to miss the bus. You can pick up where you left off back at your hotel room."

Rustling noises came from behind the stage. "Oh no, how'd they know we were here?" Candi exclaimed, sounding surprised.

"Ah—hey, thanks, dude. We wouldn't want to miss our ride." Two figures trotted out from the darkness. Candi used both hands to grip the top of her dress in order to hold it up as Jeff guided her toward the parking lot.

More laughter emerged from the two remaining couples as they made their way across the sand. "Ah, young love," Dylan teased. "Wild and crazy."

"Hey, speak for yourself. I'm not dead yet." Dave lightly patted Bonnie's behind before wrapping an arm around her and whisking her off in the direction of the exit. Dylan and Tessa overheard Dave confess tenderly to his wife, "Sweetheart, I love you more today than yesterday, but not as much as I will tomorrow."

"I love you, too," Bonnie responded with affection

then wiped away a tear as they rounded the corner and disappeared.

Dylan watched them walk away and then he took a few minutes to think about the last few hours. He had always enjoyed the company of good-looking females, but this felt different. It wasn't just fun and games anymore. He was falling for Tessa.

After witnessing the sincere love displayed a moment ago, Tessa's thoughts turned to Ben, the love she'd lost. Subconsciously, she reached up and fingered the gold chain at her throat. *I promised myself I'd try.* She had to admit this evening had been fun and that kiss—

Her lips tingled at the memory of it and her fingertips touched them lightly as heat colored her cheeks. She stood outside one of the gift shops, waiting for Dylan to return from purchasing the pictures that were taken at the entrance earlier in the evening.

He walked up beside her, smiling, eyes twinkling, and handed her a rose.

"What's this for?"

"I just wanted to thank you for a wonderful time. It was probably the best first date I've ever had."

Tessa stared at him. He didn't sound cocky or teasing. "Thank you. I had fun, too."

Dylan drove her home and walked her to the door. He gave her a sweet kiss on her cheek.

With his thumbs stuck down in the front pockets of his jeans, he sighed. "I'm not going to apologize for kissing you earlier, because it was a great kiss. I do, however, want to say I'm sorry if I crossed the line. You are a beautiful woman, Tessa. You were standing in the moonlight, and I wanted to kiss you." Dylan shrugged, hoping she would understand.

"Yes, it was some kiss. But I need you to understand my position, too. If this is going to work, you need to give me a little time." She didn't want to end the evening on such a serious note. "I do appreciate you wearing a shirt from the men's department tonight, though." She chuckled. "You look very nice."

Dylan laughed, too. They said their good-byes and he drove away.

Lying in bed that night, Tessa thought about her date with Dylan. Handsome, sweet, and sincere—a deadly combination. Every woman's dream man.

But was she ready? She thought she could do this, but now she wasn't so sure. This wasn't how she thought it would be. She shouldn't care that someone else had won the date with him at the auction or went with him to the ball. Deep down, a twinge in the center of her chest confirmed what she had feared all along.

It was too late—she did care. Tessa was playing with fire. Dylan Cooper could easily burn down the safe little world she had created. And if that happened, there wasn't enough ointment on all of Oahu to soothe the pain he could inflict upon her heart.

CHAPTER 13

I've had a lot of fun playing tourist these last few weekends," Tessa commented one Saturday morning on the way to their next adventure at Pearl Harbor.

Things had been going great between her and Dylan. They were getting to know each other better, sharing a few laughs, and a few kisses. Tessa was feeling less anxious and more relaxed about their relationship.

She was happy.

"You know, it's strange how people live near wonderful and historical sites, but never take the time to go visit them. My neighbors are retired from Phoenix, Arizona where they lived for thirty years, and they never once went to visit the Grand Canyon."

"Maybe they figured it wasn't going anywhere, and

they'd always have time to go later," he said with a straight face.

Turning her head toward Dylan, Tessa lifted her index finger to slide her sunglasses down her nose just enough so she could peer over the top rim. With a slight shake of her head, she rolled her eyes at him and his comment. "Just drive, funny man."

When they entered the visitor center complex, each rented a pair of headphones that came with a small remote. As they toured the buildings, and certain outside areas, there were designated stations that provided interesting information by punching in the corresponding number on the keypad. Tessa found the headsets to be well worth the nominal fee. There were detailed descriptions of the events as they unfolded. The couple listened to a few videos by survivors and eyewitnesses, recounting their memories of that horrible day, December 7, 1941.

The two things that struck Tessa the most were that the approaching Japanese aircraft had been detected early in the day on US radar. The report was sent up the chain of command long before the enemy planes reached the island, but they didn't take it seriously. There were some American planes from the mainland scheduled to land in next few days, and the people in charge thought the ones on the radar must be them, arriving earlier than originally planned. The other was a framed copy of President Roosevelt's speech. It was amazing to see the old-fashioned, typed pages with handwritten corrections on them, and how the famous line, "...a date which will live in infamy..." had originally been written "...a date which will live in world history..." *Not quite the same impact*, she thought.

Tessa noticed that that Dylan became more withdrawn as they continued through the exhibits. She didn't press the issue, guessing it had something to do with *his* recent memories of war.

By the time they boarded the small boat to take them out to the memorial, he hadn't said anything to her for twenty minutes.

During the short trip, she took in the scenery. The breeze combed through her hair, and the spray off the dark aqua water sprinkled droplets on her arm. Up ahead she could see the bold red, white, and blue colors of the flag popping against the sky, flying proudly over the alabaster, oblong structure that seemed to float just above the surface of the water.

After the boat docked, the passengers climbed out and then up a few metal stairs to the walkway leading into the memorial. When they entered the foyer with flags on either side, Tessa suddenly felt a light touch at her left elbow. She looked over, but nobody was there. Glancing forward, she discovered Dylan was a step or two ahead of her, so it couldn't have been him. *It must have been one of the other people on the boat passing by.* When she entered the main room, a very faint sound reached her ears.

It was a man's voice. "Welcome. Let me show you around."

She jerked her head toward the sound, but no one was standing near her. Goosebumps raced up her arms and her spine, yet she wasn't afraid. Then, as quickly and as softly as it had arrived, she felt the presence leave.

She caught up to Dylan staring out one of the glass-less windows on the right and down into the water where tons of rusted metal lay. Small rainbow-colored patches of oil shimmered on top of the water and went unnoticed by several of the visitors. At one of the information stations, it explained that, even after all these years, oil still leaked from the sunken vessel. A decision was made not to fix the issue because it would mean disturbing the site too much.

They were about to enter the room at end of the memorial, and Tessa could see a change come over Dylan. He stopped before passing through the doorway. His eyes grew dark, his face was expressionless, and his spine tall and ramrod straight. He drew in a weighted breath then proceeded into the room. Removing his cap, he respectfully stepped into the marble sanctuary. Tessa could feel the atmosphere around them intensify.

The air was different in here. Patriotism and pride became tangible things, and her heart swelled against her ribs. She approached the front and gazed in awe at the white wall with names engraved in black.

She wasn't sure she should disturb the reverent silence, but she ventured a whisper, "It's breathtaking."

She received no response, nor did she really expect one. Deep down, Tessa wanted to believe the soldiers, sailors, and Marines buried below would be proud of the memorial honoring their final resting place.

They started at the left side of the room and after a few minutes, they eased quietly to the right in order to read the next few columns. Every so often, she'd glance at Dylan's face, watching his eyes study each name, almost as if he were searching for someone. Now they were at the end. If she had blinked, she'd have missed the ever so slight catch in his breathing, before he continued until he finished reading them all.

Without a word, he turned and, just as solemnly as he'd entered, he left.

Tessa thought it best to give him a little space. She took a few pictures and stood there a little longer, studying the intricate cutouts on the walls and pondering the true price each engraved name represented. She marveled at how something so beautiful could have been born from something so steeped in sorrow.

While she waited, a woman walked in and added a beautiful yellow lei to the others draped on one of the five metal stands at the front of the room. Maroon velvet ropes hung between the posts to keep visitors from getting too close to the wall.

Just as Tessa was about to leave, three men approached the doorway, two she believed were probably the sons of the elderly man in the middle.

"I'll do it myself. I'm not an invalid," he groused.

"But, Dad—"

The older man scowled from one to the other. "The subject is closed."

The men on either side shrugged and let him have his way.

The gray-haired man, back bent from age, hobbled forward with the help of a cane. He stood in the very center of the room, as close as possible to the ropes. Tessa watched him intently. He drew in a ragged breath and, with every ounce of strength he could muster, the man lifted his head and straightened as much as he was physically able. Then slowly, he raised a trembling right hand to his temple. His face was proud, his jaw jutted forward, and his eyes were fixed and determined. The salute was short, but she had no doubt the sentiment was strong. As he turned, his misty eyes caught hers and, even though his strength had diminished, he attempted a feeble smile. "Just sayin' hello to some friends of mine."

He stumbled slightly, but held up a frail hand to her when she stepped in his direction to offer assistance, and then shot a look at the two men in the doorway waiting for him. He would do this on his own, there was no doubt. Tears stung her eyes, watching him shuffle away. She swallowed a lump in her throat before going to find Dylan.

He was leaning his shoulder against one of the openings that faced the markers designating the names of the other ships that had gone down that day. A total of eight were damaged and sunk, but only two remain buried here, the Oklahoma and the Arizona. The other six had been repaired and returned to active duty. She wasn't sure what to say or if she should say anything at all.

After a couple of minutes, Dylan casually uttered, "My grandfather." Two simple words.

"What?"

He nodded toward the end of the memorial. "He was my dad's dad."

With her hand gently resting on his forearm, she responded, "Oh, Dylan, I'm so sorry. Is that why you've been so quiet?"

"Partly I suppose. I've avoided coming here. I don't know why exactly. I guess I wasn't sure how I'd feel seeing his name up there on that wall, but not really knowing him." He faced the water, alone for a moment in the crowded shrine with his private thoughts. "I never met him, but I've heard stories about him all my life. He was a Marine. I'm actually a third-generation leatherneck. My dad was in the Corps, too. My uncles say I'm a lot like my grandfather."

She relaxed a little, watching a faraway grin play across his lips for a second or two. "Then he must've been a wonderful man."

Tessa's gaze met Dylan's when he looked at her.

"Actually, according to the family, he was quite a wild character and somewhat of a ladies' man, before he met my grandmother."

"Yup, sounds like you."

They shared a small laugh, and Dylan pulled her to him, kissing the side of her head as the tension eased. He pointed at the entrance. "Here comes a boat. Are you ready to go? I'm starving."

"Sure, but I'd like to stop by the gift shop before we leave."

Walking out toward the ramp, they passed by the flags, again.

"Goodbye, thanks for coming to visit us."

"Bye," Tessa responded automatically, adding a friendly wave over her shoulder.

Dylan paused and glanced around. "Who are you talking to?"

The foyer was empty and goosebumps once again played across her arms. "Uh…nobody. It must've been the wind."

Chapter 14

Dylan and Tessa arrived at a beach on the North Shore to watch his buddy compete in a local surfing contest. The sun was shining in a baby-blue sky dotted with a few wispy-edged, cotton ball clouds. It was another postcard perfect day in paradise.

To get a better view of the action, they walked up a grassy bank and laid down their blanket. After taking a seat, she peeled off her thin cover-up shirt and twisted her hair up into a messy bun so it would be out of the way. She applied sunscreen to her arms, legs, stomach, face, and neck. Then, handing him the tube, she asked innocently, "Can you please rub some of this on my back? I don't want to get sunburned."

His eyes drifted slowly over every inch of her now

scantily-clad body. It gave him ideas. Lots of ideas. Ones, however, he knew he couldn't act upon out here in public. As he fantasized about each steamy scenario, a mischievous smile played at corners of his mouth. Her brightly colored bikini top was tied around her neck and lower down on her back, halter style. He could see her swimsuit bottom peeking out of the waistband of her cut-off, denim shorts that rode low on her hips. Even after he'd thoroughly spread the protective cream over all the exposed areas, he made excuses that he had missed a spot or two just so he wouldn't have to stop. He loved touching her skin. It felt like satin under his hands.

Tessa closed her eyes, basking in the sensations that rippled through her while his fingers stroked her back. With each caress, her stomach quivered and quaked as if she was on a wild theme park ride. Eventually, his hands came to rest on top of her shoulders, his thumbs massaging the base of her neck with slow circular motions. Maybe she should have risked the sunburn. Her blood was already on fire from the torturously wonderful movements of Dylan's hands. If they ever took things to the next level, there was a real danger she might spontaneously combust long before they finally made love.

When she turned to retrieve the sunscreen, she discovered he'd removed his tank top, exposing his tanned chest—a seductive sight above a pair of dark blue shorts. *Oh, yeah, I'm toast.* Her eyes traveled across his bare skin as if they had a will of their own. She'd seen him shirtless before at the football game, but the sight still caused a disturbance in her heart rate.

Dylan enjoyed the sparks of want in her eyes, because he felt the same way about her. He cared about Tessa, a lot. A slow, easy smile formed on his lips, and he couldn't resist teasing her a little. Gently, he placed his index finger under her chin, nudging it upward.

A hot flush of embarrassment invaded her face. She grabbed the sunscreen and tossed the tube into her beach bag. It wasn't as if she had never seen, or been with, an attractive, shirtless man before. But Dylan rattled her. Tessa turned back toward the aqua blue ocean and exhaled. "Whew, it is *hot* out here today." Using her wide-brimmed, floppy, beach hat, she fanned herself a few times before plopping it on her head, grateful for its protective shade. Her cheeks flamed once more when she heard a low chuckle behind her. She knew Dylan found her reaction amusing. Maybe later she'd have the chance to return the favor.

They watched the contestants ride and position themselves perfectly in order to score the most points. A few of them fell off and crashed into the surf, sending themselves flying. Thankfully, nobody was seriously hurt. Some were skilled enough to maneuver their boards successfully inside the opening of a wave for a couple of minutes.

Tessa learned they called it "shooting the curl."

"I'd love to learn how to do that. It looks like so

much fun!" Her voice dripped with excitement. "Not the fancy stuff, just the basics," she clarified.

"Maybe we could take lessons. I can probably get my friend to teach us, and I should be able to get a military discount on the rental of the equipment," Dylan offered.

She smiled at him. "That would be great." She thought of something silly and snickered. "Yeah, I'll be Gidget and you can be Moondoggie." She giggled then burst out laughing.

Dylan tipped his head and squinted. "Who?"

Tessa wiped tears from her eyes and waved a hand at him. "Never mind."

After about an hour into the competition, he tilted his head toward hers. "I need to talk to you about something."

She leaned closer to him, "What?"

At that moment, the announcer was commenting on a particularly serious looking wipeout and along with the noise from the surrounding crowd, it made it difficult for her to hear.

He tried again, louder this time. "I have to tell…"

She held her hand up in the air between them. "Let's talk later, okay?" she shouted, mouthing the words slowly and with more emphasis than normal.

He didn't want to spoil this beautiful afternoon with her, so he didn't press the issue. His unpleasant news could wait. When the event was over, they took a few minutes to chat with his buddy and, although he didn't win today, they congratulated him on doing an awesome job.

Dylan tossed the blanket, beach bag, and her floppy hat in the truck, then he and Tessa grabbed a bite to eat from a nearby outdoor cafe. After lunch, they walked hand in hand along a nearby stretch of beach.

Small waves with white peaks rushed up toward them, stopping just short of where their footprints left impressions in the sand. Then, like a game of tag, the water would retreat and run back to the safety of the ocean, only to repeat its teasing and taunting a few seconds later. Tiny bubbles appeared on the sand's smooth, wet surface when the waves receded and then, as quickly as they had formed, they vanished.

At one point, Tessa drifted closer to the water's edge. She paused, lifted her face up toward the sky, and closed her eyes.

She stretched her arms out to the side and slightly arched her back, allowing her body to drink in the warmth of the sun's rays while the cool ocean bathed her feet and ankles.

Watching her, Dylan's heart swelled with love for her. Yes, he had to admit it. He loved her. A pain shot through his chest when he thought about the talk he needed to have with her.

He knew, by the end of the day, after his talk with her, tears and anger would replace the smile on her face.

He shook those thoughts aside in order to cherish the carefree, uncomplicated times they were sharing.

At this very moment, that was all that mattered. Tessa was happy.

Feeling frisky, she kicked her leg into the air, spraying him with water.

"Hey! What'd you do that for?"

She grinned. "You were looking way too serious, and I thought you needed to lighten up."

"Is that so?"

He joined her in the shallow surf and, cupping his hands, tossed water back at her. She squealed and jumped out of the way before trotting off down the beach. He chased after her, his long, powerful legs eating up the distance between them in no time. When he caught her, their feet became tangled and they tumbled to the ground.

Tessa's bare back and thighs prickled from the hot, soft sand. Dylan's solid chest lay heavy against hers. The heat from his body on top, and the beach underneath, made her feel as if she were a pair of dress pants being steamed in one of those large pressing machines that dry cleaners use.

He stared deep into her blue eyes, and the teasing that had danced in them a few minutes ago was now gone. In their place smoldered an intense, burning desire. Without saying a word, he lowered his mouth. His body ached for her, but this wasn't the place. He wasn't sure she was even ready for that kind of total vulnerability and intimacy, the giving yourself over completely to another. He'd been waiting to get her alone, to kiss her like this since he'd rubbed sunscreen on her earlier. Damn how she set him on fire, like no other woman ever had. And not just physically, but in his heart, too.

Tessa's breath caught for a second before she wrapped her arms around his shoulders and playfully nipped at his lower lip. A husky sound rumbled from deep within his chest, and their kissing quickly turned passionate with a capital "P." Hidden in a private section of the beach behind a couple of large rocks, they caressed and held each other for several minutes.

Dylan finally released her mouth only to explore the silky skin of her neck and throat. Now she was the one who whispered his name and pressed her fingers into his skin. Her hands roamed over the toned muscles of his back. An involuntary shudder sent a jolt of electricity sparking throughout her entire body when he kissed the sensitive spot along her jaw just below her ear.

Her eyes floated shut reveling in the ecstasy of his touch and his feather-light breath on her skin. Then his lips possessed hers once more with wild abandon. The ocean gently lapped against their feet and legs, enhancing the overwhelming sensations rushing through both of them.

Tessa came alive in his arms. It felt so good to be held and kissed like this again.

She heard a faint roaring sound off in the distance.

Was it her pulse throbbing in her ears? A plane flying overhead? The answer became clear in a heartbeat when a large wave crashed against them, soaking them from the chest down. The force of the water dislodged Dylan's lips from hers, and she inhaled a startled gasp. Swearing at the abrupt interruption, he rolled over onto his side with a frustrated groan.

She looked down at her soaked skin and clothes then over at him and burst out laughing.

"What's so funny?" he barked, not finding the situation the least bit amusing.

"If it wasn't for the angry look on your face, we had ourselves a Burt Lancaster, Deborah Kerr moment."

Dylan scowled.

"You know, that famous movie, *From Here to Eternity*." Tessa waved her hands around as she explained. "It took place in Hawaii and the guy was a sergeant, too, but in the Army, I think. Anyway, there's this scene where they're kissing on the beach and the waves are..." She could see he wasn't interested, or amused, by her story about some old movie. "Well, it's a classic, and it was very romantic when *they* did it."

Still, he had no response other than a grunt and shake of his head.

"C'mon, let's get out of here and get dried off." She rose to her feet and walked down to the water to rinse the wet sand from some parts of her body and brush the dry sand off the other parts.

Dylan did the same, but the cool water did little to help ease the frustration tensing through every muscle in his body. Reluctantly, he admitted it was for the best that the wave had interrupted them and kept the situation from getting out of hand. After splashing his face with water, he wiped his eyes and finger-combed his damp hair. He glanced over at Tessa splashing water up and down the body he longed to touch again, and his heart ached at the realization they might never spend another day like today together.

The worst was yet to come, and he was convinced tonight would change his life forever. And not in a good way.

A ray of sunlight pierced the water, glistening off something near Tessa's feet, as if it was purposely pointing right to it. When she reached down to pick it up, she discovered it was a seashell. She'd never seen one like it before.

About three-quarters of the shell was covered in raised ridges of black and light gray extending outward from a smooth center on the outside.

The pattern was the same on the inside except the entire surface was polished and had a mother of pearl effect, changing colors as Tessa tilted it one way and then another. Something warm spread through her chest just then, and she believed she was meant to find this particular shell. Why?

She wasn't sure because there were no other shells

around, but it didn't matter. It was going to be a beautiful reminder of her passionate afternoon with Dylan.

As they began walking back down the beach to his truck, she reached for him and placed a sweet kiss on his cheek. "Don't be upset. I loved our time together while it lasted."

He hugged her close. "Me, too."

Neither one of them said much after that. Tessa thought about the events of the day as they drove down the road, and she realized she had discovered more than the unusual shell that afternoon. She now knew, without a doubt, she was in love with Dylan. She had fought it, but no more. Joy bubbled up inside of her, and her heart felt as if it was about to burst. She wanted to blurt it out to him and to the world, but she didn't.

Tonight.

After such a great day, she would suggest they have a romantic dinner somewhere and she would tell him then. She had to do it right away before she thought about it too much and lost her nerve. She glanced over at him while he was driving and heat rose to her cheeks.

It was scary to feel this way again, but it was also, oh so wonderful. Tessa felt beautiful and sexy and wanted. She loved this man.

She loved Gunnery Sergeant Dylan Cooper, U. S. Marine.

"Are you hungry? What do you want to do for dinner?" His question broke the silence.

"I thought maybe we could get dressed up a bit and go out to a nice restaurant."

Dylan raised his eyebrows. "How about I take you home, then I'll go get cleaned up, grab a pizza, and we can stay in?"

So much for a special night out. "Sure, sounds great." The more Tessa thought about it, the better she liked the idea of having him all to herself. It would be more intimate, more private at her house. Besides, after their time together this afternoon, who knew what might happen after she confessed her love for him? *I better check to see if I have a fire extinguisher.* She blushed again, and she liked it.

An hour and a half later, Tessa paced the floor in her living room. She was excited and nervous like a teenage girl going out on her first real date. She couldn't believe how happy she was. Dylan loved her, too. Even if he'd never said it, she knew it. She could feel it in her heart every time he looked at her, kissed her.

A knock at the door startled her for a second, pulling her from her thoughts.

He walked in and gave her a quick smooch before carrying a large flat box and a plastic bag with the pizzeria's logo on it into the kitchen.

He looked good. He was clean-shaven and his skin smelled fresh from his recent shower. The cologne he wore was a combination of musk and spice that sent her senses zinging in all directions.

"One large pepperoni pizza, a dozen cheesy bread-sticks with marinara, and two Caesar salads," he announced, setting the items on the counter.

Tessa surveyed all the containers in front of her. "That's a lot of food for two people."

"I'm a big guy, and I've got a big tank to fill," he said, patting his stomach. Wrapping his arms around her waist, he lifted her off the ground. She squealed with delight while he spun her slowly a few times before returning her feet to the floor.

With his back against the counter, he kissed her softly, first her lips then her temple. He was glad she couldn't see his face.

It was time to get serious.

"I have to talk to you—" he whispered against her hair, but he was interrupted by the ding of a kitchen timer.

"I want to talk to you, too. But let's wait until after we eat," she said, grabbing a pair of potholders.

Dylan knew the longer he waited, the worse it was going to be. He had already put it off longer than he should have.

Tessa carefully removed a pan from the oven and set it on the stove. A sweet smell filled the kitchen and he smiled. "Did you make a batch of double-fudge brownies with macadamia nuts just for me?"

"Maybe," she answered, teasing him. "But I was hoping you'd share."

"I suppose," he teased her playfully, rolling his eyes, which garnered him a swat on the arm.

Tessa gathered up the utensils. "C'mon, let's eat out on the deck. It's going to be a beautiful evening."

They carried the paper plates, food, and drinks out to the patio table. He'd declined her offer of a beer. He needed to be clear-headed tonight. He knew one wouldn't affect him still, he thought it best to stick with soda.

"Hawaii really is breathtaking," he remarked, looking around at the panoramic view from her deck after they had finished eating.

"I know. I love coming out here to relax, to think, to read. It's like my own little sanctuary."

A comfortable silence gathered around them as they gazed at the ocean, the sky, and each other. Several minutes later, she took the leftover food and their silverware into the kitchen while he disposed of the paper plates, pizza box, and other trash.

When she returned, she snuggled down in his lap and draped one arm around the back of his neck. They shared a few sweet kisses. There was no need for words. *This is much more romantic than any restaurant*, she thought. It was the perfect way to finish the perfect day, wrapped in the arms of the man she loved. Now was the time. Tessa gathered her words and sat up creating space between them so she could look into his eyes.

He knew he couldn't wait, even though he didn't want to ruin this special moment with her. Why had he had put it off for so long? The answer was obvious. But at this point, he had run out of time.

It was unavoidable.

It had to be done.

Now.

"I want to tell you something—" both said at once. They each laughed nervously.

"Please, let me go first," she requested.

He relented only because she looked so happy. He knew his news would put an end to their romantic evening.

She was shaking inside, but she was so excited to finally be able to tell him how she felt. "I've been thinking a lot about us—"

Dylan's cell phone rang and vibrated across the glass top table, interrupting her. He grabbed it and glanced at the number. "It's just Mike. I'll call him back later."

"Don't worry about it. Go ahead, answer it." Tessa took a deep breath. She needed one more minute to calm the hundreds of butterflies going crazy in her stomach.

Reluctantly he agreed. "Hey, I'm a little busy right now. Let me call you back later." With one arm around Tessa's waist, he fumbled the phone slightly. Unfortunately, before he could hit the button to end the call, Mike's voice came through the speaker loud enough for both of them to hear.

"Wait. I just called to find out how Tessa took the news. How mad is she?"

CHAPTER 15

Dylan's heart sank. "I haven't told her yet," he growled at his friend who was still on the line. "But since she's sitting right here, she heard everything you said."

"Oh, man, sorry, bro. Good luck."

Dylan hung up and slid the phone across the table. He hadn't wanted it to be like this. He pulled his free hand down over his face. The joy that had shown in her eyes a moment ago was gone. In its place was a look of confusion. Tessa glanced from the phone to him and wrinkled her brow.

"What news?" She was up off his lap, glaring down at him. "What's going on, Dylan? What do you have to tell me that would make Mike think I'll be upset?"

Her head started to pound, internal alarms going off like warning sirens.

"I tried to bring it up a couple of times today, but I kept getting interrupted." He met her probing stare. "You should probably sit down."

An icy fear skyrocketed up her spine and a hammer thudded in her chest. She ran into the house. She didn't know what she was looking for, a place to hide maybe. *He's getting transferred. He's leaving Hawaii. He found someone else.* She didn't want to hear him say it. She wrapped her arms around her ribs, hugging herself tight, a protective stance and coping mechanism she'd used after Ben died.

Dylan was only a step or two behind her. "Tessa, please, sit down on the couch with me and let me explain."

"No. You should go." Reality was overrated. Maybe if she didn't let him tell her, she could pretend it wasn't true.

"I'm not going anywhere until you hear what I have to say."

"Fine, just hurry up." She plopped on the sofa, refusing to look at him. Instead, she stared at the spot on the carpet by his feet, bracing herself for the words she didn't want to hear. *Thank God I didn't tell him I loved him! How awkward would that have been?*

Dylan didn't understand why she was so upset. He hadn't even told her anything yet. He drew in a weighted breath. "There really isn't an easy way to tell you, and I'm sorry I didn't tell you sooner." He paused, searching for words that would make what he had to say less painful—but they didn't exist. "I'm leaving in three weeks. I'm being deployed to Afghanistan for seven months."

Tessa's head shot up. She saw him standing in front of her, but time stood still. *Deployed? Afghanistan?* As if in slow motion, she rose to her feet. A rush of emotions bombarded her brain and her heart. She felt his hands caressing her arms. She heard him say how sorry he was. Anger shot through her like a bolt of lightning, and she jerked free from his touch. "How long have you known?"

Dylan looked away. "Does it really matter, Tessa—"

"How long?" she screamed, hurling the words at him like daggers.

"Four months," he replied softly.

She forced her mind to calculate how long they had known each other. *He knew shortly after we met.* He had known the whole time he'd been trying to convince her to date him, even after she'd poured her heart out about Ben. A wave of fury surged within her. "So what was this between us? Just a game, something to pass the time. If that's the case, why don't you go call the tall blonde from the restaurant or Gabriella. I'm sure they'd be more than willing to 'play house' with you until you leave." She glared at him and wagged her finger in his direction. "Better yet, I think you should call the woman who *bought* you at the auction. I'm sure she'd be thrilled to get her hands on you. Again. For all I know you've bedded all three and only kept me around to fill in the gaps when they aren't available to cater to your every whim." She fired the words at him like bullets from a gun, meant to inflict a serious amount of damage.

Dylan couldn't believe she was accusing him of such things. "No! You know me better than that. I love you, Tessa."

The color drained from her face. She had planned to tell him those exact three words tonight. But she couldn't anymore. Not now, with the news of his deployment.

She speared the air with her index finger. "Shut up, Dylan! Don't you ever say that to me again!" she spat.

She tried to keep her tears at bay, but they overpowered her and she started to cry. Tessa raised her hand to slap him, but he grabbed her wrist, stopping her from connecting. Their eyes locked and the stare down began. The shock of his news and their fighting quickly drained her energy. Her anger faded, and she collapsed onto the sofa.

"How could you do this? I told you about Ben, about how devastated I was when he died." She paused to wipe the tears from her cheek. Her eyes and throat burned with regret. "You knew how I felt, but you pushed and pushed. Why? Why me?"

Dylan knew it didn't matter what he said. Nothing would make this situation better for her. "I liked you and wanted to spend time with you. I started to develop feelings for you so quickly, but they were real and they were strong. I tried to ignore them. That way when the time came for me to leave, I could go with no attachments, no strings, just like you wanted. But then, I fell in love with you, Tessa. And that's no longer an option."

"I should've listened to my head in the beginning. This is exactly why I didn't want to get involved with you or any other Marine. I start to—to care about someone, then they get deployed—then they get killed!" she yelled and began to sob.

She'd almost let it slip that she loved him, but that would have been disastrous. If he knew she felt that way, he'd never give up.

She needed to break it off with him tonight.

"Tessa, listen to me."

"No! There's nothing more you can say to make me change my mind."

Some of the bite had gone out of her voice. Mostly the hurt and pain remained. Dylan wasn't sure what drove him to do it—frustration, love. But he gambled that the woman he'd spent the afternoon with was still behind the sad eyes of the one in front of him. He grabbed her and kissed her. At first, she resisted, trying to punch his chest, but his grip pinned her arms.

The minute his lips touched Tessa's, two forces began to battle within her: anger at being betrayed by the man holding her so tightly, and love for the man who was melting her resolve with his kisses.

Her heart eventually won by the slightest of margins. When she relaxed, he loosened his hold on her. Soon her arms found their way around his neck, and she held on tight, as if she would never let him go. She couldn't believe he'd done that. She was furious but, heaven help her, she loved him too much.

After the kiss ended, Dylan continued to hug her and let her cry in his arms. They sat on the sofa in silence for what seemed like an eternity. She was scared and resentful. And he knew she had every right to be.

Somewhere in the midst of all the rage, she realized he wasn't the only one to blame for her shattered heart. She'd entered into this relationship willingly. He still shouldn't have kept his deployment from her, but she had to accept her role in this. Some of her anger faded. She'd broken her number one rule. Now she was paying the price.

Finally, Tessa reached for the tissues, wiped her eyes and nose. "You should have told me," she whispered.

"I know. I'm very sorry I didn't tell you sooner, but I knew you'd be upset." Dylan hoped he could find a way to convince her, make her understand.

She opened her mouth to speak.

"And I also know that wasn't a good reason. I should have told you as soon as I found out," he added quickly.

She loved this man sitting next to her. She wanted very much for him to be something other than a Marine. But that was what he was. Now she had a decision to make, but truthfully, there was only one choice she *could* make.

With damp, red eyes, she looked up into his face. She wanted to believe that he was truly sorry he had hurt her, but that eased the sting very little. "I wish you would have. It would've saved us both a lot of trouble."

"Would you have agreed to go out with me if I had?"

"No." Her answer was quick and unwavering.

"I'll never regret spending time with you these past months. I never thought I could care about someone as much as I do about you."

His sweet words were piercing her heart, but he had deceived her, nothing was going to change her mind.

"Dylan, I told you in the beginning about my husband and my fears of dating another Marine—"

"I know but—"

"Let me finish. If you love me like you claim you do—" Tessa almost choked on the words, her emotions were already running on overdrive. "—then I expect you to honor my decision. I can't see you anymore. I can't put myself in that situation again. I won't."

"I can't believe you're really doing this, Tessa."

"Would you rather I just play along and write you a 'Dear John' letter a couple of months from now once you're over there?"

"You wouldn't do that. You're not that kind of person."

"You're right. That's why I'm doing it now, face to

face, before you leave. I'm not going to lie and say that I don't care about you, but this is just how it has to be."

"Why do you have to be so hard-headed and stubborn?" he growled.

"Because life has taught me that if I'm not, I get hurt. And hurt badly. I refuse to let that happen."

But it was too late, she'd already let her guard down and her heart was crushed.

"What about when I get back?" He hoped maybe after she'd had time to think, she'd change her mind.

"*If* you get back, and I pray with all my heart that you do, there would always be the next deployment. Everyday I'd be walking around on eggshells waiting for you to tell me you're leaving again." Tears filled her eyes, "I can't live like that, Dylan. I won't. I'm sorry."

"I'm sorry, too, Tessa." He stood, took a couple of steps and turned back to face her. "*When* I come back—"

"Nothing will have changed." She had to make sure he understood. She needed him to realize she meant what she said.

Her eyes were cold as steel. Dylan clenched his jaw and lifted his chin. He'd known this was going to change things, but somewhere in the back of his mind, he had hoped she'd at least consider overlooking his career and giving him a chance. Obviously, he'd been mistaken. "All right, if that's how you want it." Angry and frustrated, he marched out her front door, slamming it behind him.

The pieces of her life lay shattered all around her once again. How could she have let this happen? Tessa sat on the sofa as darkness surrounded her and filled the house. She was numb and had no concept of how much time had gone by until a shiver rippled through her. Glancing around, she noticed the sliding glass door stood wide open. She shuffled across the floor to close out the night air. When she passed the kitchen, the clock on the wall chimed nine times. She must have been sitting alone about two hours.

Tessa had been a fool to listen to her heart. Love was not for wimps. How was she going to get over Dylan? Did she want to? The answer didn't matter. She *had* to. Emotions overwhelmed her, and she knew nothing was going to get decided tonight. Tomorrow she would call the only person who could help her, the one who had helped her when Ben died.

She would call Veronica. She would know what to do, what to say.

Tessa's heart depended on it.

CHAPTER 16

Tessa hurried home from work on Monday afternoon to change clothes. She, Brenda, and Michelle had volunteered to work on a fundraiser for The Wounded Warrior Project taking place this Saturday. The meeting was on base, so they met up at Brenda's since she was driving. It was more convenient for the other two, because her car had the window decals allowing them access.

When they walked into the building, the final sign-up sheets were spread across the top of the table near the door. Tessa and Brenda quickly wrote their names down to work the hamburger and hot dog booth.

"I want to sell hot dogs, too," Michelle piped up with a big grin.

In unison, Tessa and Brenda responded emphatically. "No!" They watched a disappointed frown settle across their friend's face.

Michelle glanced from one to the other. "Why not?"

With a slight shake of her head, Tessa raised her eyebrows. "Way too dangerous."

It took a minute for the words to register, but then Michelle grinned. "Oh yeah, 'cuz I'd call them wein—"

"Yes." Brenda hushed her with a look that would've made any experienced mother proud.

Tessa tried to sooth Michelle with a compliment. "Lisa mentioned she'd like your help with the decorations and signs. She knows how creative and artistic you are. The day of the benefit, Meg said she would appreciate some help in the face painting booth for the kids. Besides, it'll be safer for the Marines this way."

Everyone around them laughed, except Michelle. She sulked and pouted for about twenty minutes. *Now, I won't be able to flirt with any of the hunky single guys.*

After a short speech by the event organizer covering basic information, they split up into smaller groups and met with the chairperson assigned to each booth or activity for more detailed instructions.

∞∞∞

Early Saturday morning, people carried ice chests, in all colors and sizes, full of food, drinks, and snacks from the parking lot. Shades with a tent-like top sprang up all around the perimeter of the grassy park. There were also some with the fabric enclosing two or three of the sides. These helped block out the breeze and gave the vendors more vertical selling space. The volunteers, Marines, and merchants scurried around getting everything ready for the festivities. The scent of charcoal and delicious-smelling, barbequed food soon infused the air.

Ear-piercing noises from military jets screamed overhead off and on throughout the day. Trails of white slashed through the blue sky like a knife through an artist's canvas.

Business had been steady. At some of the busiest times, the lines were five and six people deep. Tessa greeted all the customers with a smile, but eventually their faces blurred together.

For the last half hour, Dylan stood a few feet off to the right and watched her, but he didn't think she'd seen him. Maybe it was time he changed that.

With a quick swipe of a damp rag across the make-shift counter, Tessa didn't even look up at her next customer. She automatically repeated the question she had been asking all day. "What can I get for you?"

"That's a loaded question." His deep chuckle held a hint of teasing.

Her head snapped up and her heart pounded against her ribs. "Hello, Dylan." She hadn't seen him since he stormed out of her house after their fight. She stared at him for a second before glancing away. Part of her was happy to see him, because she'd missed him. Although she was still struggling with the hurt, she couldn't deny the fact that she loved him.

"How are you?" he asked.

She wouldn't look at him. "Fine."

She busied herself restocking the plastic baskets with small packets of mustard, mayo, and ketchup. A couple of short, blonde stands of hair blew across her face and became entangled in her eyelashes.

His arm instinctively twitched, wanting to lift his fingers and brush them back behind her ear. But he didn't. He knew she wouldn't welcome his touch.

Annoyed, she swiped at her hair and repeated her earlier question.

"Two burgers with the works, fries and a soda, please," he said.

Tessa tallied his order and handed him the change from the twenty he'd given her. She was totally oblivious to the other noises around her as she watched him walk away.

"Oh. My. Goodness," Michelle cooed.

Her announcement startled Tessa, and she jumped at the sudden appearance of her friend. "What are you doing here?"

"I just came by to ask Brenda a question, and I'm glad I did." Michelle nodded her head in Dylan's direction. "He looks just as yummy from the back as he does from the front. Umm, umm."

"This is why we didn't let you have direct contact with the adult male customers," Tessa reminded her with a soft grin. "I'm sure the Marine Corps wouldn't appreciate their legal staff being buried under mountains of paperwork. It would take months for them to sort through all of the sexual harassment charges filed against you if we'd let you work the counter. Now scoot."

Michelle knew her friend was only teasing, but that didn't stop her from taking another peek over her shoulder at Dylan before she disappeared.

Tessa continued to help the other customers. She would sneak a glance over at Dylan every once in a while. He'd always catch her peeking and toss her wink or a wave. She would quickly blush and look away.

It was late afternoon when Tessa, and the other ladies, started packing up the booth. All of a sudden the excited shouts of a small child filled the air. "Uncle D! Uncle D!"

A rosy glow colored the boy's fair cheeks, no doubt the result of his time spent enjoying the outdoor activities at the park this afternoon. Boundless energy still seemed plentiful—arms pumping at his sides and short little legs scurrying as fast as they could go. With each step, baby-fine, white-blond hair floated in the air around his head, rising and falling like silk threads, as soft curls bounced near his neck.

A huge smile broke out across Dylan's face at the sight of the youngster.

Within three feet of the Marine, the child stopped and looked down at the ground. With a great deal of effort and concentration, he lined up his red sneakers side by side, just like he'd been taught. When he finished, the boy gazed up into the face that towered above him, stuck out his little stomach, and placed his tiny fingers alongside his temple. "Private Timmy reporting, sir."

It was all Dylan could do not to burst out laughing. He glanced around and found the child's mother standing a few feet away, watching her son. Tears glistened in her eyes, but there was an unmistakable glow of pride on her face.

Dylan cleared his throat, stood at attention, and returned the salute. "At ease, Private."

Timmy let his arms hang at his side.

The Marine put both of his hands behind him, casually placing one inside the other and resting them against his lower back. He walked around the boy in a mock inspection.

"Have you been doing your chores, Private?"

"Yes, sir," a little voice boomed.

"Have you been obeying your mother, Private?"

The youngster sighed and peeked over at his mom. She raised an eyebrow, but added a nod and smile.

"Most of the time, sir." His voice didn't hold quite the same conviction of his previous answer.

"Do you promise to work on that before next inspection?"

"Yes, sir."

"But if you neglect your duties or are insubordinate, I have instructed your mother to call me. Understood?"

Timmy lifted his scrunched-up face. "In-sa what?"

Dylan bit back a chuckle and leaned closer to his little friend. "It means if you don't behave."

"Oh, okay." The child sighed again, knowing he didn't want to get in trouble with his mom *and* his Uncle D. *Man, it's just so hard to* always *follow the rules*.

"All right then, you're dismissed, Private."

The man and the boy exchanged salutes one more time. Timmy had barely taken a step in the direction of his mother when Dylan reached down and scooped him up, tickling him, and flipping him upside down. Timmy squealed in delight. Setting the child's feet back down on the pavement, the Marine ruffled the boy's soft hair, held his small hand, then joined the little guy's mom. Dylan gave her a hug and kissed her cheek.

He squatted in front of the boy. "I'm going to call next week and if I get a good report, I'll come by and take you out for ice cream. Deal?"

A huge smile exploded on the youngster's face, "Deal!"

His little arms flew around his Uncle D's neck, hugging him tight. The child's mom thanked Dylan before taking her son's hand and wandering out of sight.

Tessa witnessed the entire interaction. She felt a twinge of jealously, watching the affection between the man that had flirted with her earlier and this other woman.

"That's Jodi and her four year old son," Brenda informed Tessa. "Her husband is deployed right now, and Dylan promised he'd check on them."

A whirlwind of emotions and thoughts rushed through Tessa. Dylan had shown such tenderness to Timmy and his mom. He didn't speak baby talk to the child, but talked to him with love.

She chuckled softly to herself. Maybe next he would save Lassie from a well or a kitten from a burning building. He seemed almost too good to be true. Then she remembered the day at the beach. His smile had made her heart pound and his kiss set her blood on fire. Now, on top of all that, he was great with kids. Every other sound around her faded. All she heard was the hammering of her pulse, as she thought about the man she loved.

Her heart didn't stand a chance.

❧❧❧

Later that evening, everyone met at the baseball field. The tall, overhead lights illuminated the players, bathing them in the warm glow of a cherished summer pastime. Since the game was organized only a week ago, there were no uniforms.

One team wore yellow T-shirts while the other team wore red.

Tessa, Michelle, and Brenda found seats on the metal bleachers among the rest of the spectators. They were mostly the wives and girlfriends of the Marines, and a few of their kids played in the dirt nearby.

Standing at home plate, the umpire flipped a coin. The yellow team won the toss, and they chose to bat first. Dylan and Mike, along with the rest of their teammates in red, were designated as the home team, so they took their positions on field.

The score went back and forth, which kept the game exciting. Michelle did her part to distract the players on the opposing team by calling out to them as they ran the bases. "You go you sexy thing!" she yelled. "After the game, maybe you can meet me under the bleachers."

One of the players on the yellow team tripped over first base because he was flirting back with her and not paying attention to where he was running. The other coach complained after the third inning and the umpire told Michelle she had to knock it off. Mike and Dylan had already warned her about doing that to any of the guys on their team.

By the sixth inning, frustration among the players on the yellow team had started to show. They expressed their opinions of the quality of the ump's calls quite loudly, along with a few choice swear words thrown in for good measure. On the very next pitch, the ball came a little too close to their teammate's head. He threw down his bat, pointed at the mound, and began yelling. The pitcher said it was an accident, but the batter didn't find the apology sincere enough. He charged the mound. Immediately, all the other players on both sides ran for the infield to participate in the bench-clearing brawl that ensued. It resembled a pack of hungry dogs rushing to fight over a single scrap of meat. Some players tried to break up the fight, while others swung wildly at whoever got in their way. The spectator's reactions varied from boos to gasps, to yelling and cussing at the players. Finally, the fight ended and everyone returned to their positions on the field or back to the dugout.

At the bottom of the ninth, the score was tied. Mike hit a double and stood on second base. Dylan was up next. He paused by the bleachers along the third-base line, a flicker of arrogant amusement in the flirty, half smile he aimed at Tessa.

"I just thought I'd let you know, I'm gonna hit a homerun just for you."

After he left, he whipped his ball cap around backward on his head and took his place on the right side of the catcher.

Tapping the bat twice against home plate, he kicked at the ground and pivoted the toe of his left cleat into the dirt before assuming his well-honed stance. The pitcher glanced over his right shoulder at Mike, standing on second base, then released the ball.

Dylan didn't swing.

A hollow thud sounded as the ball hit the center of the catcher's mitt.

"Strike!" the ump shouted.

Dylan stepped out of the batter's box. He tapped the bat against the inside edges of his cleats, more out of habit than necessity. Encouragement from his teammates and the stands filled the air.

"Come on, you can do it," Brenda cheered. "Bring Mike home."

Tessa cheered for Dylan throughout the game but kept her emotions mostly on the inside, expressing only a clap now and then. Earlier, he'd made a great catch and a throw that saved at least two runs from scoring. Now, watching him up to bat, she saw the muscles in his arms flex tight against his shirt. Those were the same strong arms which held her so tenderly and lovingly not that long ago. Today was more difficult than she'd thought it would be.

Stepping up to the plate, he repeated his routine. The pitcher threw the ball toward home and once again, Dylan made no attempt to swing.

"Strike!" the ump called again.

The opposing team jeered. "He can't hit the broad side of a barn."

"Just one more, Mitch."

"You got this, Big D!" Mike hollered.

Right before Dylan began his at bat ritual, he glanced

over at Tessa and winked. He smirked as he readied himself for the next pitch. His plan had worked. The pitcher
looked overconfident and that was a big mistake. As soon
as Mitch released the ball, everyone held their breath. A
loud crack echoed through the air and powerful biceps
catapulted the ball as if it had been shot from a gun.
There was no doubt in anyone's mind—they knew it was
gone. Dylan ran the bases and looked up just in time to
watch the ball easily clear the fence in center field. His
cheering teammates met him at home plate to congratu-
late him with slaps on the head, back, and shoulders.

Tessa couldn't help but smile. She was happy for
him. He was making it very difficult for her to resist him,
no matter how upset she was at what he had done. She
had a feeling that had been his plan.

When Dylan's teammates finally let him go, he strutted over to the bleachers. Most of the people had left the
area, and Brenda congratulated him before going to find
Mike. Michelle had wandered off, hoping to find a player
on the losing team that might need comforting. Dylan
hung his fingers through the heavy chain link fence between him and Tessa.

She smiled. "That was quite impressive."

"I told you I'd do it. And I always keep my promises,
Tessa."

She looked at him skeptically. "You couldn't possi-
bly know you were going to hit a home run."

"Sure I could. I've played baseball since I was in Little League and continued all the way through high school. I'd been watching the pitcher. He's young and cocky. He also had a couple of beers in between innings, so I just let him think he had the skills to throw me out."

Tessa thought for a moment. "You're pretty sure of yourself, aren't you?"

"I know what I want and I go after it."

Her insides trembled at the huskiness of his voice. She saw a determination and desire in his eyes that had nothing to do with baseball. It was too intense to continue staring at him, so she bent down and grabbed her tote bag.

Tessa cleared her throat. "Well, good game and nice hit. I better catch up to Mike and Brenda, they're my ride."

"I'd be glad to drive you home," Dylan volunteered.

Her brain was screaming no while her heart was pleading yes. Tessa needed to stick by her decision and start the healing process.

It wasn't going to be easy.

Thankfully, her friends showed up, and she didn't have to answer.

"You ready, Tessa?" Brenda asked.

"Yup. Today was fun and we raised a lot of money for a great cause, but I'm tired." She looked back toward the fence for just a second. "Bye, Dylan."

After the three left, he gathered up his gear. Tessa didn't appear to be as mad as she was the other night, but he saw the lingering hurt still in her eyes when he offered her a ride home.

Dylan knew if he had some time, he could fix this. But he didn't have time. Yet, he had to believe there was still hope he could convince Tessa to reconsider her decision before he left.

He just had to.

CHAPTER 17

Mike and Brenda invited Tessa over for dinner a few days after the baseball game. Mike was like a brother to her. And she loved him like one. He was always there with a big hug and a "Hey, cutie." He knew how to make her smile. And that meant a lot to her.

She was still feeling a little down about Dylan, and she was smart enough to realize this invitation was their attempt to get her out of the house. Still, she was looking forward to a good home-cooked meal. Tessa didn't enjoy making food for one. Most of her dinners came from the drive through or the microwave. After setting the table, Tessa helped with the last minute preparations, and then the meal was served.

The food was delicious and the conversation was pleasant. Her friends made sure to avoid the subject of *him*. She'd just finished helping Brenda clear the table when they heard the front door open and close.

Mike poked his head around the corner of the kitchen, "Hey, Tessa. Can I talk to you for a second?"

Puzzled, she looked over at Brenda, who suddenly avoided Tessa's gaze by concentrating on the contents in the back of the frig. After wiping her hands dry on a dishtowel, Tessa tossed it on the counter and walked out into the living room.

There stood Dylan.

Her eyes darted to Mike's, "What's going on? What did you do?" Her voice grew more unsteady with each question.

"Tessa, just listen to me," Mike started. "You two need to talk, and I know how stubborn you can be, but time is running out."

She couldn't believe Mike had betrayed her. "How could you do this? Brenda, get out here." *Was she in on it, too*?

When her friend appeared in the doorway, the answer was obvious. The sheepish look on Brenda's face told Tessa that she knew about this the whole time. Tessa didn't even need to ask.

Mike tried again. "Tessa, you know we love you." He pointed back and forth between him and his wife.

"You had no right—"

"I *do* have the right. As far as I'm concerned, you're family. Besides, Ben was my best friend." Mike's tone was a little harsher than he had intended, but it got her attention. And this time, he wasn't going to let her interrupt him. "It's killing your friends to see you not truly living your life. Dylan loves you. And we all know that you love him, too. Please just sit down and talk to the guy. Maybe give yourself permission to love someone again. I know Ben would want you to be happy. And you are *not* happy. You're trying to deny your feelings for Dylan or use excuses, no matter how valid, to push him away. Enough already."

Tessa was stunned that Mike was speaking to her this way. Especially in front of Dylan. Yet, no matter how mad and hurt she was, she had to admit there was some truth in what he had to say. Spearing the space between them with her index finger, her eyes narrowed slightly.

"You may be right, but you still shouldn't have called me on it. Not like this."

"Would you have agreed to meet him any other way? He leaves in a few days, Tessa. You both deserve to figure this out before then."

She looked over at Dylan.

His hands were shoved down in the front pockets of his jeans. He shot Mike a sharp glance. "I'm sorry. I thought you knew I was coming over. I did want a chance to talk, to clear the air. And, Mike's right, time is running out, Tessa."

The words were said with sincerity, but not a hint of pleading. Tessa knew Dylan would never beg her to love him. His pride wouldn't allow it.

And she wouldn't want or expect him to.

Brenda finally spoke up. "Tessa, we might not have handled this in the best way, but I agree with Mike. We love you and we're worried about you. Can you at least talk to Dylan? Mike and I will give you some privacy."

"If you'd feel more comfortable at home, we could talk there, Tessa," Dylan offered.

She looked into the three faces in front of her. The will to fight was slowly evaporating. Turning around, she plopped into a chair at the dining room table, a palm cradling her forehead. She had so many emotions running through her mind at the moment clouding her, otherwise, good judgment.

"All right, Dylan, let's get this over with."

It was going to be a difficult conversation. She would be drained when it was over. Tessa had no doubt he would ask her if what Mike said was true. She wouldn't be able to deny it. She believed he already knew, anyway. He'd seen it in her eyes. She loved him.

Now Dylan would only lobby harder for them to be together.

Tessa looked over toward Dylan as a weary breath escaped her lips. "This might take a while, so I think it might be best if we go to my place." She stood up, grabbed her coat, and spoke calmly over her shoulder to

Mike and Brenda. "Thank you for the wonderful dinner. I know you meant well, but you shouldn't have interfered." She paused. "Please don't ever do it again."

⌘⌘⌘

A few minutes later, Dylan followed Tessa into her living room. "Thanks for agreeing to talk."

Without turning around, she responded, "Since I was ambushed, I didn't really have much of a choice."

"Tessa, I'm not here to start a fight."

"I'm sorry. I don't want to fight either." She'd missed him so much, but it was complicated. And she didn't want complicated. Unfortunately, it was too late. She was in deep.

"I'd hate to leave with the way things ended between us a couple of weeks ago." Dylan's voice was calm . There was no anger or bitterness in his tone.

She didn't want to rehash all the reasons she decided not be with him. It hurt to be with him, it hurt to picture her life without him. "Dylan, I really don't think there's anything left to say. I'm sorry we fought, but I'm—"

"Mike was right, wasn't he?"

Staring out the window, Tessa swallowed down the anxiety building in her throat. She'd known what he was going to ask her.

"About what?"

"I've known for a while, but I would like to hear you

say it." Dylan went and stood beside her, turned her to face him. "Tell me, Tessa."

For just a moment, when he looked at her like that with those bedroom eyes, he could almost make her forget all of her fears. She didn't deny him the simple request. Staring at him, she whispered, "I love you, Dylan."

Strong hands tenderly held her face as his thumbs caressed her cheeks. With his lips less than an inch from hers, their breath mingled together as he responded with a raspy voice, "Oh, Tessa, I've waited for you to say those words."

Her hands found their way around his neck and they hugged and kissed for several minutes. She finally realized this wasn't the reason they'd come here, and it wasn't solving their problems.

"Wait," she said breathlessly, pushing him away. "We came here to sort things out, not *make out*." She saw a smirk start to form on the same lips that had just sent electricity sparking through her. "And even though that was a fun interruption, *you* were the one that wanted to talk."

Dylan knew he couldn't push too hard or joke around. Tessa hadn't appreciated being set up tonight. He'd better lay his cards out on the table and play it straight. "You're right. Let's go sit on the couch." Once they were settled, he began again. "I love you, Tessa. Sometimes those words come with high expectations or commitments the other person isn't ready for. You don't have to worry about that. There are only a couple of things I would like to ask of you." He paused, seeing apprehension on Tessa's face. "I'd like you to wait for me. Also, please don't make any sudden and permanent decisions about our relationship while I'm gone. When I get back, I'd like us to start dating again and see where it goes. I don't have any doubt that we're meant to be together, but I know you do, and I also know why. Could you please do these things for me?"

Tessa's insides were trembling, and she folded her arms across her stomach. She searched Dylan's face. His expression was so hopeful and sincere. In reality, he hadn't asked for much. But from her, he'd asked for the one thing she didn't think she could give him—to trust him with her heart, to have faith that her world wouldn't be turned upside again. "I don't know. I'm afraid," she answered, hesitantly.

"Afraid of what?"

"You," she whispered as tears filled her eyes.

Dylan was stunned and deep lines creased his forehead. "Me? Why? I'd never hurt you."

"You could die. I love you and you could die."

He reached for her hand. "You're right. But that could happen here in Hawaii, too."

"But this is different. You are putting yourself in danger on purpose. Why should I plan a life with you? I gave up believing in the magic of fairy tales and happily-ever-after. Then you came along and reminded me of how good it felt to be loved, desired, kissed, and held. I don't want to feel like that and have it taken away again. It's too much pain, too much hurt."

Dylan's eyes challenged her. "Do you think you're the only one who will suffer? Don't you know how much I'll miss you? Your kisses? I'm having a difficult time thinking about saying goodbye to you, too. But this is my job and this is how it has to be. For now, I'm government property."

"And if they wanted you to have a girlfriend, they would have issued you one," she said, half-teasing and half-spiteful. It was a stupid, old military joke, but it popped into her head so she blurted it out.

Dylan stood, went to the kitchen, and poured himself a glass of water. When he returned he stood in front of Tessa. "You know, I'm proud to be a Marine. A few guys join, do their time, and get out. But a lot of us take it seriously. We are a family, and we develop a bond most civilians have a hard time understanding. Semper Fi isn't just a motto we use or words to be thrown around lightly." He tapped the center of his chest. "Real Marines feel it, deep down inside. For me, it's a code by which I chose to live my life—Always Faithful. I'm dedicated, Tessa. I'm dedicated to my God, my country, the Corps, and to the people I love."

"How do I know that you won't change your mind after you come home? How do I know I can trust you with my heart?"

"Because I'm giving you my word." Dylan's voice was clear, the words spoken with pride.

Tessa studied his face. She wanted to believe him. She wanted to believe his love had the power to erase her fears. But it would cost her so much, especially if he failed at his keeping his promise. Looking at him as tears burned behind her eyes, she nodded. "I'll try," she whispered.

"That's good enough for now." He held out his hand to Tessa and they walked to the front door. "I'd like to take you out to dinner the night before I leave."

"Okay."

Dylan pulled her into a warm embrace and whispered in her ear, "It will be all right. I'll make it worth your wait when I get back."

Tessa could feel him smile against her temple.

And she prayed with all her heart he was right.

CHAPTER 18

Dylan and Tessa had gone out to eat at one of their favorite restaurants. Soft music played in the background, and candlelight danced around them in the intimate corner booth. For the last twenty minutes, she'd just sat there, pushing her food around on the plate with her fork.

Despite the romantic ambiance and savory cuisine, she didn't have much of an appetite.

He reached across the table and caressed her hand. "Is something wrong with your dinner?"

"No, it's fine." As his thumb gently stroked her knuckles, she knew his concern was genuine and sincere. Dylan Cooper was a good man. A fact she'd realized not long after they had started dating. He had everything a woman could hope for in a man. "I'm sorry I'm not very good company tonight."

Dylan understood her mood reflected the fact he was leaving tomorrow afternoon. He smiled, trying to lift her spirits. "Don't worry about it. Do you want to go to a movie or maybe go out dancing?"

She stared into his deep brown eyes and handsome face. Two very different, and conflicting, emotions rose up in her—a powerful ache in her heart and a sensual flutter in the pit of her stomach. "Not really. If you don't mind, I think I'd like to go home." She saw a momentary flash of disappointment flicker across his face. Glancing down into her lap, she twisted the cloth napkin in between her fingers. "It's still early, you should go meet up with some of your friends. At least that way, the evening won't be a total waste."

"I don't want to spend time with them, Tessa. I want to spend time with *you*," he said, his tone firm, but kind.

She wished he wouldn't place so much emphasis on trying to make these last few hours extra special. Didn't he understand that every sweet thing he did, every time he made her laugh, every romantic moment they spent together would only make it that much more painful to say goodbye at the end of the night? And, why did he have to be so charming? He said all the right things and looked at her with those incredibly sexy eyes. Eyes that made her want him, made her forget he was a Marine— made her forget where he was going tomorrow.

After Dylan paid the bill, the two walked out to his truck. They rode in deafening silence the entire way to Tessa's house. The radio wasn't even on. The only sound she heard was the hum of the tires on the asphalt. He pulled up in front of her house a few minutes later. Even though she hadn't invited him in, he walked her to the front door, following her inside. They had talked several times since that evening Mike and Brenda had ambushed her, but he hadn't been back to her home.

"Would you like some coffee?" she asked softly, flicking on the lights before hanging her coat in the entry closet.

"I don't want you to go to any trouble."

"No big deal. It's one of those one-cup-wonders," she said on her way to the kitchen.

Dylan could feel the tension between them continue to build the closer the time came for him to leave. When Tessa brought him the coffee, he asked, "Do you want to go sit out on the deck?"

"Not really."

"Do you want to go walk on the beach?"

"No thanks."

Bending his elbows slightly, Dylan raised his palms toward the ceiling. "Tessa, what can I do to make this evening better?"

She didn't want to fight again. No questions. No over-thinking. No talking about tomorrow. "Nothing, I'm fine."

"The hell you are!" he snapped, his patience running out. "I want us to enjoy each other's company tonight. I know it's difficult—"

Scowling, she spun around to face him. "What do you want me to say, Dylan? That I love you and I'll miss you? All right, fine. Yes, of course I will. But I don't want to talk about tomorrow. I don't want to talk about the future. I just—I don't know."

"I thought we had come to an understanding the other night, but it seems I was wrong. I've made no secret of how I feel about you, Tessa. I love you and want you in my life. Ignoring the issues, and pretending they don't exist, only makes things worse. Maybe we *should* clear the air between us again, if that will help."

Tessa glared at him. "Thank you, Doctor Freud, for your keen observation, but I disagree. Now is not the time to—"

"When will it be? I leave in less than twenty-four hours."

"Stop it, Dylan. I'm not going to stand here, in my own home, and be bullied or guilted into making you promises I can't guarantee I'll be able to keep. If you're trying to push me by forcing the issue the night before you leave, it's not going to work."

Rubbing the back of his neck, he started to pace. "What is it that you want from me? Tell me what I can do to make you change your mind about me. About us."

"I want you to *not* be a Marine leaving for Afghanistan tomorrow." A combination of anger and fear could be heard in her voice. "I want to *not* be scared every minute that you're gone." With a wave of her arms, she pointed her index finger at the TV. "I want to be able to watch the news without being afraid your name and face will pop up on the screen when they show the latest casualties. I want you to be a plumber or a dentist or an accountant." Her voice softened. "I want you to be *anything* but a Marine leaving for war tomorrow." Her shoulders sagged. "I want you to promise me you won't die."

Tessa tried to be strong tonight, but one lone tear broke free and trickled down her cheek.

Dylan took her hand gently in his, gazing deep into her blue eyes. "I know, but I *am* a Marine, and I can't promise you that I won't die." He spoke softly. "I *can* promise you that I will do everything in my power to come back home to you."

Studying his face, she saw the tenderness in his eyes and knew he meant every word. She felt it every time he kissed her and by the small, intimate ways he had touched her when they were alone.

"I'm not trying to upset you or complicate your life. But I need you to know how much I love you before I leave. Just in case…" he said, lowering his voice.

The impact of the words he didn't say hit her hard, like a wrecking ball destroying everything in its path. Memories rose up, choking her, cutting off her airway, and Tessa closed her eyes. She understood all too well "just in case" was a very real possibility. Still, a part of her refused to acknowledge that scenario and she pushed it from her mind. "I'm sorry, Dylan. I don't want to fight with you. Not tonight." They hugged each other tight, sharing an unspoken love and forgiveness between them. "Do you have time to stay and watch a movie with me before you have to leave? I'll make sure it's a comedy." Tessa didn't want him to walk out her door.

Not yet.

He glanced at his watch. "No, sorry. I better be going. There are some last minute things I need to pull together." Dylan lifted his hands and cupped her face. "I need to kiss you one more time, Tessa, a kiss whose memory will carry me through the next seven months."

She felt the warmth of his body and the strength of his muscles as he held her. Her eyes swept across his lips before gazing up into his tanned, chiseled face. "That's a lot of pressure to put on one little kiss, don't you think?"

A familiar, roughish grin appeared. "Maybe, but I have faith in our kisses. I know we're up to the challenge."

Heat replaced amusement in his eyes as he leaned down and pressed his lips to hers. It was tender at first, then desire took over, along with his overwhelming need to burn every detail into his memory. Passions flared. They both understood the importance of this one last kiss.

When they separated, Tessa felt weak, desired, and loved.

Reluctantly, he reached for his coat. "I'll try to keep in touch, but I'm not sure how often that will be possible. So don't worry if a few weeks go by before you hear from me."

"That's a promise I know I can't make," she replied, her voice cracking.

For all of her rants and determination, something erupted in her—something urgent and undeniable as she watched him walk away from her. Tessa understood she was playing with fire, but right now, she didn't care. The inevitable pain of reality would be here soon enough. He had just reached for the doorknob when she called out to him. "Wait. Would you—I mean—" she sputtered. "Could you please spend the night?"

Dylan's eyebrows shot up. He was shocked by her question. "I don't think that's such a good idea." He couldn't believe he was turning her down. When he saw the reaction on her face, he hurried to explain. "Don't get me wrong. I'd love to stay. I've thought about us— together—more than once. But tonight might not be the best time for us to—"

Tessa blushed slightly. "Oh no—I don't mean that. I know it might not make sense, but I was hoping we could just hold each other and talk about nothing important." Biting her bottom lip, she continued, "I know it's a lot to ask, considering our recent circumstances. Just because I'm scared doesn't mean I don't love you. I need you to- night, Dylan." When he didn't answer right away, she rushed to withdraw her request. She shook her head, embarrassed she'd even brought it up. "You know, never mind. It was a crazy idea."

He wasn't sure he could lay next to her all night when his mind would be consumed with the overwhelming desire to make love to her. Tessa had no idea what she was asking of him. Yet, the more time he could spend with her, no matter how torturous, would be better than nothing. Besides, he knew if he walked out her door, regret would rob him of any sleep he had hoped to get tonight. Without breaking eye contact, he reached up and secured the deadbolt.

She hadn't really expected him to agree to her proposal. But she was happy he did. "Let me go change clothes. I'll only be a minute."

Dylan smiled, trying his best to be the calm, suave, worldly man he portrayed himself to be while his insides were auditioning for Circ de Sole. "No rush."

He removed his coat and tossed it over the back of the couch. Silently he gave himself a pep talk while pacing the floor. *You can do this. Just keep your hormones in check. You've slept with a woman before and not had sex. You can do it again.*

He didn't have any protection with him, so he knew that would help deter him from succumbing to his desires and letting things go too far. As much as he wanted to be with her, he knew she wasn't ready. He took a deep breath and readied himself for battle—a battle of testosterone and lust versus respect and love for Tessa. The self-discipline and fortitude he'd learned from his numerous hours of grueling combat training would never be more useful than it would be these next few hours.

Tessa's voice called from down the hall. "Dylan? You can come in now."

She might feel guilty about her offer by the harsh, accusing light of day, but not tonight. Tonight, she needed him, needed his strength to help her face tomorrow. She needed him to stay with her and convince her everything was going to be all right.

"Well, here goes nothing," he whispered and flipped off the living room lights before heading in the direction of her voice. He removed his shirt and shoes, but left his jeans on. They laughed a little, talked a little, keeping their conversations light. Drifted off with her in his arms, he felt like this was where he belonged—here with Tessa.

There was a feeling of contentment and security in having a man's body snuggled up against hers. She had missed that. She hadn't realized just how much until right now. There was also fear, knowing that it was a very real possibility she would never have him lay beside her again.

Her last thought evoked a feeling of emptiness. It was the reason she'd fought so hard against letting him in her life in the first place.

Tessa stayed awake for a while after Dylan's even breathing indicated he'd fallen asleep. He was the first man she'd cared about since Ben had died. A mixture of emotions fought for space in her mind. Remnants of anger and hurt lingered from the night they fought and the night she agreed to try. She prayed she could make it through these next long months.

But she was tired now—tired of fighting, tired of worrying. Her heart reluctantly waved the white flag of defeat. She'd lost the battle and had no choice but to surrender. To love. Hopefully, this time, it wouldn't let her down She closed her eyes and concentrated on the rise and fall of Dylan's chest, letting the even rhythm lull her to sleep.

ఴఴ

When the alarm woke them the next morning, neither of them wanted to face the fact that he had to leave. But now, the unavoidable had arrived.

"Thank you for staying," she whispered against his skin.

He leaned over and placed a soft kiss on her forehead. "I'm glad you asked. I liked waking up with you in my arms."

A few moments later, they got out of bed, and she disappeared into the kitchen. While Dylan was putting on his shirt, he surveyed the various bottles of perfume on Tessa's dresser. Picking them up, one by one, he took a whiff.

"What are you doing?" she said, walking back into her bedroom. "I don't think any of these are quite right for you."

"Ha. Ha. Are you always so funny first thing in the morning? I'm looking for the one you usually wear. The one you wore last night."

Tessa reached for a uniquely shaped bottle with a pink tint and handed it to him. She watched him unscrew the top, put the opening near his nose, and inhale.

"Umm, yup, that's the one." As he closed his eyes, sensations tickled his stomach—and constricted his heart. Pulling in another long breath, he noticed her staring at him. "I'm just taking one last sniff. Seven months is a long time."

"Well, I may be able to help with that." She walked out of her bedroom, and when she returned, she was carrying a small, craft size, plastic bag plus a pair of scissors.

He raised an eyebrow. "What are those for?"

"You'll see." She opened the bottom drawer of her dresser and lifted out a red silk negligee. She saw Dylan's eyes open wide as she lowered the sheers.

"Wait! Don't do that, you'll ruin it."

"No worries. It was a gag gift from Michelle for my last birthday."

Tessa wearing that red nightie was a picture he would have a difficult time deleting from his memory, but his racing pulse changed his mind. It was an image

Dylan would gladly carry with him. He watched her cut a small heart shaped piece from the nightie. Picking up the perfume, she placed the red scrap of fabric over the opening and tipped the pink glass bottle upside down. Tessa waved it back and forth in the air a few times before placing it in the plastic bag. "I don't know if you can keep this in your pack, but if you can, here's a heart to carry with you while you're gone."

He stared at her, surprised, considering her attitude lately. Still, he was very touched by her gesture. "I'll pin it inside my uniform." He placed her palm against the center of his bare chest. "Right here," his voice was low and raspy. "When I get lonesome, I'll pull this out, smell your perfume, and think of you, knowing you're right here with me."

She could feel his heart beating beneath her hand. Tears clouded her eyes. This big tough Marine loved her—really loved her.

"Now, I have something for you." He slipped off his Marine Corps ring, placing it next to the black and white souvenir she found on the beach after the surfing contest. "I remember how excited you were when you found this shell, and you were concerned it would get broken before you made it home." They both chuckled. "So I'm going to leave my ring here with you for safe keeping, and then I'll pick it up when I get back. When you look at it, you can think of me, and know a part of me is always with you."

Tessa knew she didn't need a shell or a ring to remind her of him. Every minute of every day, her heart would make it impossible to forget him.

After one last passionate kiss goodbye, Dylan left. Wondering if she would ever see him alive again, Tessa pressed her back against her front door. She slid down the cool, wooden surface to the floor, and pulled her knees up to her chest.

After placing her face in her hands—she wept.

Wept for the man she loved.

CHAPTER 19

Tessa found the non-descript, gun-metal-gray building without much difficulty. Carefully studying her watch, she approached the designated side door and knocked, like she'd been instructed to do. Tap, tap, tap. Pause. Tap, tap.

As if by magic, it opened and she slipped inside, with a little help from Mike, her co-conspirator. She had called him right after Dylan left.

"Thank you," she whispered.

"Are you sure you don't want to go tell him goodbye in person?"

Her hand gripped his forearm. "Please, you can't tell him I was ever here," she pleaded then dropped her gaze. "It's—it's complicated."

"Anytime there's love and a woman involved, complicated isn't far behind."

Her eyes narrowed as she looked up at him. "Oh and you guys are such peaches to deal with." She chuckled slightly and nudged him with her shoulder. "C'mon, take me to the window."

They walked a few yards and then made a left. Down at the end of that hall, Mike slowly tried the handle. It was unlocked.

He motioned her in and quietly closed the door behind them. The room was small and dimly lit.

An old metal table and six matching chairs sat in the middle, taking up most of the space. Everything was painted the same dingy gray as the outside—the walls, the furniture, the built-in shelves, as well as the concrete floor.

Keeping her voice low, she waved her hand. "Does the Marine Corps have something against color?"

"What?" Mike glanced around. "Gray's a color," he said, his tone matter-of fact.

Tessa rolled her eyes. Her friend nodded toward the small window in the corner, opposite from the door.

"Now remember, no lights, no loud noises, and don't touch or lean on the glass," he said, his voice lower and more serious. He saw fear transform her face.

"I thought you told me nobody could see in and that it was covered with that reflective film on the outside?"

"It is, but sometimes, depending on the position of

the sun, I've heard guys say they can see shadows or movement if a body is right up against it."

Tessa nodded.

"When I come back for you, we'll have to go. You have to blend in with the other civilians. If for some reason you get caught before I get back, just tell them it's your first time on the base and you got lost."

"Okay. I really appreciate this, Mike."

It was his turn to nod then he left her alone. Her stomach was churning with nerves. She had decided after Dylan left her house earlier this morning that she needed to see him again—but on her terms.

Inching up closer to the window she peered out, but kept a safe distance like Mike had recommended.

Marines carried bulging duffle bags to what looked like a staging area stacked with other gear they would be taking on deployment.

Tessa observed some of the men standing around in clusters. Some were laughing and pretending it was just another day, but their body language made her believe it might only be a coping mechanism to cover up their anxiety. Others huddled together with family and friends, smiling and joking, trying to keep their emotions at bay for a little while longer.

A few, with their cover shielding their eyes, found a quite spot to catch a couple extra winks, no doubt after a late night of partying. Or could it be that watching others share heartfelt goodbyes was too difficult when they had no one there to embrace them with a hug or to wish them a safe return.

It was as if Tessa had been punched in the stomach. Her breath caught and she closed her eyes. *That describes Dylan. He isn't going to have anyone to hug him good-bye.* Tears burned in her eyes from the guilt of hiding in this room instead of showing him how she felt. But, she'd said her goodbyes in private. Out there, it could get messy and that wouldn't be good for either of them. Especially in front of his men. Her eyes snapped open when she heard two males stop next to the window of her secret hiding place. She froze, afraid if she moved further into the shadows, they might see her.

A loud voice shouted outside and the two men moved away. Tessa waited until she felt it was safe enough to sneak closer for a better look. The Marines had their backs to her and were lined up in rows, like they would be for an inspection. She scanned the large sea of green cammies and there, off to the side, facing the group, was Dylan.

An ache spread through her heart. He looked so handsome, so professional, so serious, but sad around his eyes. Tessa's body tingled with the memory of his arms around her, tight, yet tender. The simple feeling of her hand in his while they'd walked down the beach. And the heat of his lips on hers.

Slowly, she touched the tips of her fingers to her mouth. He stirred such desire inside of her. She swallowed a lump that threatened to choke her. Releasing a heavy sigh, she straightened her spine.

She knew she was doing the right thing, but that didn't stop her from wanting to run outside, leap into his arms, and kiss him with all she had.

But she wouldn't.

She couldn't.

Noises once again pulled her back to the scene outside the glass. The men were dispersing. They were ready to leave.

Families gripped their loved ones and tears streamed down several of the sad faces. Tessa felt a few of her own roll down her cheeks.

Dylan? Where is he? Frantically, she searched the faces in the crowd for him. *There!* Just a few feet away stood the man she loved. Slowly, she lifted her fingers to trace his image on the tinted windowpane, but stopped just in time.

She couldn't risk being discovered.

A soft click startled her. "Tessa, it's time. We've gotta go," Mike whispered from the doorway.

"Please," she choked out, "one more minute. I'm not ready to lose him yet." She prayed Mike didn't hear the last part of her plea.

"Sorry. We have to go. Now." His tone was gentle—but firm.

Slowly, she backed away from the window and joined him.

"Are you glad you came?" he asked, wondering if he'd made a mistake in agreeing to bring her here. He could tell she'd been crying.

She sniffled and forced a grin. "Yes."

"Are you still sure you made the right decision by not saying goodbye in person?"

This time, Tessa could only nod when she met her friend's gaze. She didn't even bother trying to deceive him by attempting another artificial smile.

Retracing their steps from earlier, Tessa gave Mike a quick hug before he opened the metal door that led outside. "Thanks," she said softly in his ear.

The bright sunshine flooded over her as if she was under a spotlight. Squinting tight, she retrieved her sunglasses from her purse then carefully walked around the side of the building and joined the other people heading to the parking lot. Behind her, she could hear the diesel engines of the buses starting up. They would transport Dylan and the rest of the Marines to the planes on the other side of the base. Tessa sat in her car a minute, trying to pull herself together enough to drive home. Being here this morning had affected her more than she thought it would. But she didn't regret coming.

After she arrived home, she worked around the house, trying to keep occupied, especially if it involved physical labor. She swept, mopped, vacuumed, washed windows, anything to help keep her mind off the events of earlier.

Hours later, lying in her bed, she finally gave in and allowed herself to cry over Dylan. She missed him so much already. How in the world was she going to survive the next seven months? Reaching across to the empty spot next to her where he'd slept, she wondered if she'd made the right decision not to make love with him. She wasn't sure, because now she longed for his touch and his kiss. But what if they had and what if—

What if? Two small words. The "what-if's" would drive her crazy if she didn't get them under control in the beginning. But Tessa knew very well what havoc they could bring into a person's life if they were allowed to run wild.

Sleep was elusive that night. She was restless, catching only short naps here and there. She woke up several times and reached for him. Finally, she grabbed the pillow he'd used and hugged it tight. It still smelled of him. It seemed to calm her and she eventually drifted off.

The next morning, she knew she needed to sort out what was on her mind. Memories of Ben had made surprise appearances into her dreams last night and that only enhanced her feelings of despair. Maybe if she wrote down her thoughts it would help.

She took out a notebook and started writing. Before long it turned into a list, a comparison between Ben and Dylan. Tessa could feel her anxiety level rising rapidly. This wasn't working. Yet what she found was that they were similar in a lot of ways. Maybe that's why Tessa had fallen in love with each of them. They were both handsome, sweet, kind, and loving. Dylan had more of the overt, macho, in-your-face-alpha-male attitude. Ben was all man, but he didn't feel the need to publicize it as much. Ben had been about six foot and Dylan stood six-two. Both men loved her and she loved them.

She'd buried one.

And she was terrified she'd have to bury the other.

Why hadn't she stopped this sooner? She knew better, but it was done. There was nobody to blame but herself. Nobody had forced her. Nobody had tricked her. She'd willingly bought a seat in this game of chance. She'd gambled and gone all in. The price to play—her heart. But after the cards were dealt, she'd realized there was no winner. She'd come out the loser either way.

She loved Dylan so much and it scared the hell out of her.

Scared that she would let him stay in her life. Scared that she wouldn't.

But how could she have let herself fall in love again that deeply?

And especially with another Marine?

CHAPTER 20

Pinned down by enemy fire, Dylan and his squad could hear the bullets whiz past them as they fought to hold their position until help arrived. Powerful explosions sounded in the distance, yet they were close enough to make the earth rumble beneath their dust-caked boots.

"Perkins, get on the radio and call the command post. Find out where the hell our damn air support is!" Dylan could hear the sergeant emphatically explaining the seriousness of their situation.

A string of colorful curse words flowed from Perkin's mouth, causing Dylan to turn toward him.

"They said it would be at least a half an hour until they can get here, Gunny."

"What?" Dylan bellowed, concerned the delay could mean some of his men might not make it out of here alive.

Twenty more minutes went by and the fighting hadn't let up. "Corporal O'Donnell, how's our ammo supply holding out?"

"Unless things take a turn for the worse, we should be good for a couple more hours, Gunny."

"Keep me posted, Corporal," Dylan shouted.

In the next heartbeat, he felt a burning in his chest and shoulder. A searing pain ripped through him, like being stabbed with a red-hot poker. He'd been hit—knocked onto his back in the sand.

A few seconds later, small puffs of dust floated in the air around him.

He felt himself being dragged closer to what was left of a nearby building. Someone was putting pressure on his chest then he heard his sergeant yelling.

"Hold on, Gunny! Perkins, grab the radio and call for a medivac. Now!"

Dylan lost track of time, floating in and out of consciousness. He opened his eyes just as the fighter planes flew overhead, their silhouettes dark against a bright blue sky.

The help they'd needed had finally arrived. After about ten minutes, there was a break in the gunfire. In the momentary silence, the whirling sound of a Huey could be heard.

"Your ride's here, Gunny. Only a few more minutes, okay? Hang in there!"

Thompsons's voice started to fade as Dylan's eyelids floated shut. Suddenly, the image of a beautiful blonde appeared in his mind. Would he ever see her again? Would he ever kiss her again? A soft, unnoticed whisper escaped his lips. "Tessa."

Then his world went black.

∽∾∽

Back in Hawaii, Tessa had had a difficult time falling asleep the night before. She'd been worried about Dylan.

She'd made the mistake of watching the evening news, even though that was something she usually tried to avoid. The last time she'd glanced at her alarm clock, the bright red numbers glowed in the darkness, 2:30 am. She rolled over and must have drifted off, because before long Dylan's face wandered into her dreams. They were walking hand in hand on the beach laughing, smiling, and enjoying the gentle ocean breeze. She could feel the soft, warm sand under her feet and the sun on her face. He stopped abruptly and looked at her. The expression on his face scared her. His eyes were cold and dark.

"Dylan, what's wrong?"

"I have to go." His tone was even but serious.

"What do you mean *go*?"

As he stepped back, she noticed a red stain blossom in the middle of his chest. She gasped when she realized it was blood. It soon spread outward, covering the front of his white T-shirt. In the next second, he vanished like a wisp of smoke on the wind.

Panic gripped her heart, and an eerie chill surged through her entire body. She screamed his name and bolted upright in her bed. The room was dark and her heart was pounding. Pulling her legs up to her chest, she rested her head on her knees and cried for several minutes, giving in to the overwhelming emotions that engulfed her. It was only a dream. But it had felt so real, and it had terrified her.

Her clock now read 5:00 am. Unfortunately, it was Wednesday and she had to go to work. She really wanted that extra hour, but Tessa knew there was no way she could go back to sleep now after that nightmare. Throwing back the covers, she staggered to the kitchen and made herself a cup of coffee before shuffling off to the bathroom to take a shower. Maybe she could get a little housework done before she had to leave. She knew when she got home tonight, she'd be exhausted. Her plan was to shut out the world and hopefully, fall right to sleep—and not dream.

❧❦❧

When Tessa left work on Friday, she felt relieved the

weekend was finally here. Tomorrow, she planned to sleep in, stay in her PJs, and not leave the house. A do-nothing-kind-of-day. It wasn't something she did very often, but her body and mind were telling her it was time.

When she arrived home, she went straight to her bedroom, changed out of her business clothes, slipping into a pair of her comfy shorts and a T-shirt. A quick snack of cheese and crackers from the kitchen would have to serve as dinner. She plopped herself down on the sofa and clicked on the TV. *Let the hours of mindless relaxation begin.* Flipping through the channels, she found an old movie she loved. But before long, the characters on the screen weren't holding her attention like they usually did. She began to feel a little uncomfortable, inside and out, so she tugged at her shirt and adjusted her shorts. She even tried crossing her legs underneath her. It was her favorite "couch-potato" position, but nothing seemed to help.

Popcorn.

Tessa went into the kitchen, tossed a bag in the microwave, waited for the ding, and then poured the steaming white puffs into a bowl. She resumed her place on the sofa and her attention back on the movie. Twenty minutes later, her mind began to wander once more, and her restlessness intensified.

She stood up and roamed around the house looking for something to do

After throwing out what was left of the popcorn, she

added the bowl, along with a couple of forks lying in the sink, to the rest of the dishes in the dishwasher.

She needed something to occupy herself until this sense of uneasiness passed. Tessa had no idea why she felt this way, but she couldn't seem to shake it. Walking by the bookcase in the living room, she spotted the latest romance novel she'd purchased last week. She carried it over to her favorite blue, overstuffed chair in the corner and wiggled her butt down in the seat cushion. She'd finished three pages, then tugged at her clothes, and squirmed slightly to find just the right spot in order to concentrate. After another two pages, she released a frustrated groan and fidgeted with the pillow at her back. She was determined to give it one more try.

Tessa was actually able to make it through five pages this time. However, she wouldn't have been able to tell anyone a thing about what she'd just read. Finally, she closed the book and slammed it on the side table.

Rising to her feet, she walked to the kitchen and opened the sliding glass door. Out on her deck, she inhaled deeply and let the cool, tropical air fill her lungs. She leaned against the railing and gazed into the evening sky. A multitude of stars were on display. Some of heaven's sparkling crystals winked down at her as they lay scattered across an unending canvas of black. A soft yellow crescent moon dangled among them. It was so beautiful here. She couldn't imagine living anywhere else.

As her mind began to relax, an unexpected theory

emerged in her thoughts. Could her restlessness have anything to do with that awful nightmare she had about Dylan last week? But that didn't make any sense. It was, after all, just a dream. And she wasn't even thinking about him when these feelings had started earlier this evening. Could he be looking at this very same moon? Tessa did some quick calculations in her head and realized that wasn't possible because of the time difference. It was sometime Saturday morning in Afghanistan. She didn't take the time to figure out exactly, but she had a general idea of the time difference. Her thoughts remained on the man thousands of miles away. Where was he right this minute? Was he in danger?

A surge of panic clutched at her chest. Trembling, Tessa sent up a silent prayer for Dylan's safety. At that exact moment, her anxiety began to fade. Calm and peacefulness took its place. She felt the tension drain from her body as if warm water was cascading slowly down over the top of her.

Closing her eyes, she tried to understand what had happened tonight. Her thoughts and feelings were all jumbled and had been for months. Odd things she couldn't explain had occurred ever since she'd met Sergeant Dylan Cooper, very odd indeed.

After drawing in one more deep breath of refreshing night air, and with one last look at the beautiful starlit sky, she went into the house, locking the door behind her. She strolled back to the corner of the living room, and this time she discovered her favorite chair was miraculously more comfortable than before. Tessa started reading her book again—from the beginning.

❧❧❧

A balding man in a white medical coat stepped up to Dylan's bedside. The doctor adjusted his glasses and flipped through the top three pages of the chart to scan the latest entries. "Morning, Sergeant Cooper. I'm Dr. Brooks, the surgeon that operated on you last week. How are you feeling today?"

Dylan winced, trying to push himself up into a more comfortable sitting position before answering the man with the stone-faced expression. "A little better, sir. Thanks for patching me up."

"The truth is, Marine, if that bullet had been an inch closer to the center of your chest, I doubt we'd be having this conversation. I was told you were wearing a vest, though. Is that right?"

"Yes, sir. But sometimes they start to wear out before we get newer ones. And then sometimes—" Dylan motioned toward his chest. "Sometimes, an enemy bullet just gets through."

The older man nodded. "Well, it was touch and go for the first couple of days. It didn't look good. You had us worried, son. We couldn't seem to get you stabilized, and you were going through a lot of blood." The doctor

removed his glasses and stared at Dylan before he continued. "Medically, I can't explain it, but all of a sudden
Saturday morning everything just came together and it
worked out in your favor." He gave Dylan a lop-sided
grin. "You must have one hell'va guardian angel looking
out for you, Sergeant Cooper."

Just then, Tessa's beautiful face appeared in Dylan's
mind. "Yes, sir," he whispered. "I believe you might be
right."

Chapter 21

Around 3:00 am Wednesday morning, Tessa was sound asleep when an irritating noise penetrated her dreams. Mostly out of habit, she flopped her arm over in the direction of her nightstand and slapped at the snooze button.

But the annoying sound didn't stop. Struggling to wake up, she managed to lift one heavy eyelid, and that's when she realized it wasn't her alarm. It was her cell phone. She grabbed it, pressed it against ear, and rolled onto her back. Half-heartedly, she muttered a groggy hello.

"Is this Ms. Tessa Matthews?" the unfamiliar female voice inquired.

"Yes." Even though she was tired, Tessa's instincts

went on full alert as she tried to come up with a reason why anyone would be calling her at this hour. It was rarely to relay good news.

"My name is Linda Hill. I'm a Red Cross representative with the hospital here at Ramstein Air Force Base in Germany. I'm calling about Gunnery Sergeant Dylan Cooper. He was seriously injured, but his recovery is going very well and he's currently in stable condition. He requested I place a call to you just in case you had heard or seen anything on the news."

The shock of hearing those words jolted Tessa awake instantly. She flung her legs over the edge of the bed as an icy panic seized her heart.

She swallowed hard, fear forcing a lump to rise in her throat. "Oh no! What happened?"

"Sergeant Cooper was shot twice, once in the shoulder and once in the chest. He was air-evacted here to the hospital."

Tessa leaned her elbows on her thighs and held her head in one hand.

This was so much to absorb. A variety of emotions erupted inside of her. "How long has he been there?"

"Let's see…" Ms. Hill paused while she flipped through the patient's information. "He arrived here a week ago today, so that would make it early Wednesday morning your time. I do apologize for calling at this early hour, but my shift is almost over, and then I will be leaving for two weeks. I've been working with Sergeant

Cooper and he specifically requested that I be the one to call you. He can be very persistent and stubborn."

Both women chuckled slightly.

"Please let him know how sorry I am that he was hurt, and that I'm very grateful he's going to be okay."

"I most certainly will, Ms. Matthews."

"Thank you so much for calling. I really appreciate it." But before Tessa hung up, she clicked on the light next to her bed just long enough to ask the woman for the hospital's mailing address so she could send Dylan a card.

After placing the phone on her nightstand, she turned off the lamp. Sitting there in the dark, she could feel the tears welling up inside of her, stinging her eyes until they spilled over her lashes and streamed down her cheeks. She cried, not only because Dylan had been hurt, but also because of how much it scared her, and because of how angry she was at herself. This was the very reason she didn't want to get involved with him in the first place. She loved him, but love wasn't always enough.

Long after the call ended, and her tears had ceased to flow, Dylan's face stayed in Tessa's thoughts. She finally lay back down and, although the room was completely dark, she soon realized sleep was no longer a possibility. Something the woman from the hospital said kept nagging at her. Tessa threw back the covers, walked over to her desk where she kept her "memory book," and switched on the small lamp. It wasn't a diary or a journal really, because she didn't write in it every day. She only used it to jot down special thoughts or ideas. Tessa opened the book and began to page through it. She came to an entry with the same date as the one Ms. Hill had mentioned. The date Dylan had been shot. Tessa thought she was going to faint. That was the day she'd had that dream—the one with them on the beach. The one where Dylan had disappeared after his shirt became covered in blood. Shocked and trembling, she stumbled her way back across the room and plopped down on the edge of her bed. Her mind was spinning.

Could their connection really be that strong?

Was this some kind of sign that they were meant to be together?

c⌐oc⌐o

Dylan shuffled across the tiled floor. There was a phone call he needed to make. A call he'd wrestled with, and one he had talked himself out of making a half a dozen times, but it couldn't wait any longer. For a few moments, he wanted to reach across the miles and hear her voice. Talk to her, if for no other reason than to let her know he was doing okay. He hoped she'd be glad to hear from him, too.

A few days after she'd received the call from the Red Cross representative, Tessa was busy at work. She needed chocolate, and fast. It had been that kind of day. It was absolutely a full-sized candy bar crisis—fun-size was not going to cut it. She doubted the medical community would agree with her, but she definitely considered the silky, brown sweetness a medicinal substance. There was a forty-five cent discrepancy in the spreadsheet she was working on in her office. Right before lunch, she'd spilled coffee all over the monthly report she had spent all afternoon yesterday working on.

Grabbing a bunch of paper towels, she had sopped up the caramel-colored liquid the best she could. She picked up the soaking-wet printouts with her index finger and thumb, shaking coffee into the garbage can. After the second or third page, she realized she might as well just toss the unsalvageable report into the trash, along with the soaked paper towels. Thankfully, she could reprint the report and add a few handwritten notations.

About two o'clock in the afternoon, her cell phone rang. She didn't recognize the number, but she needed a break from staring at her computer screen, so she answered it anyway.

"Hello."

"Hey there," a tired male voice greeted her.

"Dylan?" Tessa's pulse quickened and her stomach muscles fluttered at the sound of his husky tone. She was so glad to hear from him. She'd missed him. "How are you?"

"I've been better," he said, grinning slightly against the receiver.

"I can imagine. The Red Cross called and told me you were in the hospital. What happened?"

"I don't really remember much. I know we were taking on heavy enemy fire. I think my sergeant called my name. Suddenly, I got slammed into the dirt and then saw blue sky." He paused, wondering if he should confess that his last conscience memory was of her, but he decided against it. "Then things went black and I woke up here."

Leaning her head back against her office chair, she closed her eyes and shuddered as if caught in a cold gust of wind. "Oh, Dylan, how horrible. I can't imagine what must have gone through your mind."

A moment of silence lay between them before he responded. "I've been thinking a lot about you, especially since I've been here."

The sound of her voice brought a rush of memories to his mind. How her silky, honey-blonde hair felt against his skin, the soft smell of her favorite perfume, and the special twinkle in her deep blue eyes when she laughed.

"I've been thinking about you, too," she whispered. She wished she could reach through the phone, touch him, and kiss him. Remembering her dream again, Tessa's chest began to ache. Silence returned for a few more seconds. "Are you still in a lot of pain? How much longer do you think you'll have to stay in the hospital?"

"The pain is pretty manageable at this point. They had me on some really heavy-duty stuff when I first got here. The doc says a couple more weeks, and I should be good enough for them to ship me home. I'm ready to get outta here."

"I'm sure you are." Tessa glanced down at her watch. "What time is it there? Shouldn't you be sleeping?"

"It's about one o'clock in the morning, but I'm tired of lying in that bed, so I sweet talked one of the nurses into letting me use the phone for a few minutes," he said with a slight chuckle.

Tessa knew that his charm and sexy good looks could get him whatever he wanted with most women. "I'm sure you probably didn't have to try too hard," she teased. They talked a few more minutes, but she could sense the weariness in his voice. "I should probably let you get some rest."

"Yeah, I suppose. The nurse is looking over here with a concerned 'mother face.'" He paused, before asking her the question that had been on his mind all day. His heart was hoping she'd say yes, but his head was trying to stop him from getting his hopes up. He had a good idea of what was about to happen, especially under the circumstances. However, he couldn't rest until he asked. "Tessa, if I email you the date I'm coming home, will you be there?"

"I—um—" Tessa stuttered. She hesitated, trying to come up with the right words. "I'm not sure if I can promise you that, Dylan. I'm sorry. Your getting hurt really scared me. I—I just don't know." Squeezing her eyes tight, she felt a few silent tears burn a trail of guilt down her cheeks, but she swallowed a whimper, not wanting him to hear her cry.

Didn't he understand that just hearing his voice was tearing her apart? Her emotions were in a tailspin. It was too hard to love him, but yet so easy. It was all she could do not to scream into the phone that she loved him and missed him, and that she would still wait for him. "I thought I could do this. I know this doesn't make things right, but I tried, Dylan. When you got shot, all the old fears and memories came rushing back." Her voice was cracking as she squeaked out the words.

He could feel the muscle in his jaw tighten, he was so disappointed. "I'll let you know anyway, and then you can decide later. But I'd like you to at least think about it." His tone was firmer now than when they'd started their conversation. Dylan Cooper had never begged a woman for anything before in his life, but this felt pretty close. And he'd never do it again. "I'm getting kinda tired now. I better get back to bed."

She knew she'd hurt him, but she didn't want to make promises she wasn't sure she could keep. "Of course. I hope you feel better. Goodbye, Dylan."

Waves of sadness, mixed with a little anger, pulled at his heart. But he knew there was nothing more he could do to change her mind, especially from a hospital bed thousands of miles away in Germany. Tessa loved him.

Unfortunately, *his* love just might not be enough to convince her to give them a real chance for a future together. He shouldn't have been surprised. She had always been up front with him.

꽃

Tessa couldn't sleep that night, thinking about Dylan's phone call. She was so thankful he was going to be all right. The more she dwelled on her feelings for him, the more upset she became. How long was she going to straddle this emotional fence she'd been teetering on for months? She knew she was being selfish and unfair to Dylan—and to herself. He deserved better. Dylan could have very easily been killed, and she would have had to endure all of that pain and grief again like she did with Ben. She should have listened to her head in the beginning.

Now, she had to answer to her heart.

Tessa knew she had probably sounded cold on the phone. That wasn't what she had wanted. She was just trying to protect her world from shattering into a million pieces. She'd never survive another military funeral. Hanging her head, she wept at the thought of hurting the man she loved—again.

But the question remained. He'd asked her to come see him when he came home. Her head pounded and her hands began to shake as a whole new set of questions popped into her brain.

She knew the answers would affect the rest of her life.

Would she be strong enough to go?

Would she refuse his request?

Would she be able to stay away?

CHAPTER 22

Tessa and Brenda were having lunch at one of their favorite little cafés downtown. After they both ordered the soup and salad combo, they talked until their food arrived. Tessa seemed preoccupied and kept fidgeting around in her chair.

"What's wrong with you?" Brenda asked finally.

"Dylan called me from the hospital in Germany yesterday."

"Really? How's he feeling?"

Pushing her fork around in her Caesar salad, Tessa shrugged. "Okay, I guess. Well, I mean as good as can be expected, under the circumstances."

"That can't be the reason you're acting restless. What else did he say?"

Silence filled the small space around them for a moment. "He asked if I'd be at the base when he comes home."

"You *are* going, right?" Brenda's tone implied she didn't actually expect an answer, especially not the one she received.

Tessa lowered her head. She could feel the pressure building behind her eyes. "I don't know if I can."

"Why not?"

Tessa shook her head but didn't say anything.

"I know you love him, so what's stopping you?" Brenda asked bluntly.

Tessa lifted her gaze to meet her friend's impatient stare. "Yes, I love him, but sometimes that's not enough to make a relationship work. Besides, it doesn't matter. I—"

"Of course it matters. It's all that *should* matter."

"Just because I love him doesn't change the fact that I can't be with him, build a life with him."

Brenda arched her eyebrows and lifted her palms toward the ceiling "Because…"

"He's a Marine," Tessa responded wide-eyed and matter-of-fact, as if the answer should've been obvious.

Brenda had finished the last of her soup and the spoon was still in her hand. Waving it around in the air between them, she used it like an extension of her index finger. "Yes, he is. He was when you met him, when you agreed to go out with him, and when you kissed him."

"The stakes are just too high. You know I can't risk going through that again."

Sitting back in her chair, Brenda exhaled her frustration as the spoon slipped from her fingers, clattering inside the empty, ceramic soup bowl. "You know, that line is wearing a little thin."

"Excuse me?"

Tessa couldn't believe her friend had spoken to her like that. Anger and hurt welled up in her because this person, who was supposed to be one of her best friends, was being so insensitive.

Brenda saw the wounded expression her words had caused. "Listen, you know I care about you, but I'm tired of you using that as a reason to run away any time there's a bump in the road with Dylan. He's a great guy. He loves you and you love him. I don't understand why you won't give him a real chance to make you happy. Don't you love him enough to take the risk? Can you just write him off and move on? Can't you see a future with him?"

"Look what just happened!" Tessa's emotions were so frazzled, she couldn't control them. Her voice rose an octave or two and she slapped her hand on the table. "Isn't that proof enough?"

People around them in the restaurant turned to stare in their direction.

Panic and tears filled Tessa's eyes. Brenda reached over to cover her friend's hand with her own. She hoped the gesture, along with the concern in her quiet response, would help calm Tessa. "And from what Mike said, he's going to be fine."

"But what about next time? What if he's not so lucky? You don't understand the pain I went through with losing Ben. I don't ever want to feel that way again. I dealt with it for a long time. Now Dylan comes along and resurrects those fears and feelings. I love him and I'm scared to death I'm gonna lose him, too." She paused, and when she spoke again, it was through trembling lips. "Then what will I do?"

"Then you'll deal with—just like you did before—and be thankful for the time you two had together. Veronica, Michelle, and I will be there for you. Mike will, too."

Shocked, Tessa glared at Brenda. "I don't know how you can say that to me! You saw what I went through. I don't know if I could survive something like that again."

"You could if you had to. You're stronger than you think. And if anybody has the right to talk to you this way, it's me. I *do* understand what it's like to be married to a Marine."

Tessa closed her eyes for only a second or two, as the feelings of guilt pinched her conscience at the way she'd spoken to her friend.

"You're right, of course. I'm sorry, Brenda. But aren't you terrified every time Mike goes on a mission or gets deployed?" she asked, her voice softer now.

"Every second of every day," Brenda choked out the words. Her emotions were making it difficult for her to speak.

Staring at her friend, Tessa's anger faded when she looked into the damp hazel eyes across the table.

Clearing her throat, Brenda continued, "I don't want to think about what my life would've been like without Mike these last few years. We cherish each day we're blessed to share with one another." She dabbed the corners of her eyes with her napkin. "So now *you* need to decide what you're going to do. He'll be home soon."

"I know," Tessa muttered.

The waiter walked up and asked if they would like any dessert. When they both declined, he cleared the dishes and left a small black folder containing the bill. Brenda insisted lunch was her treat. She slipped enough cash inside to cover the amount, plus a sizable tip.

Before they got up to leave, Brenda, once again, laid her hand over Tessa's and looked deep into her eyes. "You know, the more I think about it, the real question you need to answer is not whether you can see yourself happy *with* him for the rest of your life, but whether you think you can live the rest of your life and be happy *without* him."

Fear and reality joined forces and sent shockwaves jolting through Tessa. Her body trembled at the significant impact and power in Brenda's words. However, it didn't make her decision any easier.

Either choice could rip her apart.

Brenda offered her a comforting smile. "Just follow your heart."

Tessa sighed. "That's easier said than done."

☙❧

Dylan eased himself down onto his hospital bed after taking a stroll outside in the fresh air. Just as he was settling under the covers to take a short nap, a cute, young nurse standing across the room offered him a flirty smile.

She waved a couple of envelopes in the air as she made her way over to him. "Sergeant Cooper, some letters came for you today." When she handed him the mail, her fingers came in contact with his. Sparkling green eyes twinkled under her long, dark eyelashes. "Would you like me to fluff your pillows?"

The top button of her crisp white uniform was undone. Obviously, it was her not so subtle plan to ensure that, when she leaned over, he had an up-close view of her cleavage. She also made every effort to leave a lasting impressing on her return trip to the nurse's station. He had to admit that she looked just as good walking away from him as she did walking toward him. Dylan smiled, but he wasn't interested in her. A few months ago, he'd have played the game she was offering. But not now.

His heart belonged to only one woman, and because of that, so did the rest of him. That thought drew his attention back to the letters in his lap. He flipped through them one by one. The first was from his mother, the second from his younger sister, and the third—was from Tessa. He set the other two aside. His heart thumped a little faster in anticipation as he opened the envelope. A picture of a Hawaiian sunset and palm trees decorated the front of the beautiful card. Opening it, Dylan scanned the left side of the card hoping for a personal heartfelt message from Tessa, but he was disappointed.

It was blank.

He read the handwritten words that were penned under the pre-printed Hallmark get-well sentiment.

> *I hope you feel better soon.*
> *Take care, Tessa.*
> *P.S. I'll have an answer for you when you*
> *get back.*

He let out a weary breath and carefully slid the card back inside the envelope. "Well, I guess I have no choice but to wait and see what she's going to decide," he whispered to himself. Even though Tessa hadn't said "No," he read between the lines. He wasn't going to get his hopes up about their future together.

About that time, the over-attentive nurse strolled back to his bed. "You look upset." She nodded toward the mail. "I hope you didn't get one of those awful 'Dear John' letters."

He was in no mood to deal with her at the moment. "I don't feel like company right now, sorry. I'd like to get some sleep."

The young woman looked disappointed but she didn't say anything before walking back to the nurse's station. Placing the envelopes on the little side table, Dylan laid his head on the pillow and closed his eyes. He wasn't sure how much sleep he would get after reading Tessa's card.

He had hoped for better news.

℮৲ℑ℮৲ℑ

The entire time he'd been gone, Dylan often roamed in and out of Tessa's thoughts. Randomly and unannounced. But since he'd been hurt, every time she walked by her dresser, she felt as if there was a huge, blinking, neon arrow hanging from her ceiling pointing directly down at the black and white sea shell she'd found on the North Shore. Normally, she was able to ignore that small, but powerful, reminder of the one day that held the best, and the worst, memories of her time with the man she loved.

Today was different somehow. It was as if a force she couldn't explain was drawing her to it. Gently, she lifted the shell and examined its beautiful intricate details. She turned it over in her fingers, letting her skin graze across the two extreme opposite textures. Her thumb skimmed over a silky smooth inside. It had a mother-of-pearl effect, but the colors were mostly light gray with a hint of purple. The center on the outside of the shell was similar to the inside in color and feel. From there, rough ridges formed a stripe-like pattern, starting half way down and spreading outward to the edge.

Tessa couldn't help but smile as she held the keepsake. It reminded her of Dylan. He was a big, tough, macho Marine on the outside. His pride and ego ran as hard and deep as the black and white groves. But on the inside, he was kind, caring, compassionate, and loving. The memory of him with the little boy at the Wounded Warrior Project benefit was the perfect example. Recalling that day, she chuckled lightly as the images danced in her mind's eye.

Returning the shell to its place on her dresser, Tessa walked out of her bedroom and through her house, ending up out on her deck.

She could think there, clear her head. Her smile quickly faded as she thought about the decision she had to make. An ache in the center of her chest soon followed.

Dylan would be home in a couple of days. What was she going to say? She needed to give him an answer.

He *deserved* an answer.

Looking up into the clear blue sky, Tessa spoke softly. "Oh God, I don't know what to do. I've fallen in love with a man who could tear my world to pieces. Although he won't do it intentionally, I'm so scared. I'm scared he'll die like Ben did. Won't you please take away these feelings I have for Dylan? I don't want to love him," she pleaded desperately. Months of tears and joy, pain and happiness that had been battling for space inside of her began to pour out. "God, why? Can't you see what this is doing to me? Why did you bring Dylan into my life?"

A still, soft voice, not audible, but one deep down in her spirit, answered her. *To help heal your heart.*

At that moment, a powerful feeling of love washed over her. Tessa leaned against the railing and wept. As her tears flowed, she released all of the guilt, fear, and heartache.

She stayed outside for another hour, crying and thinking, while the warm ocean breeze dried her cheeks. Things became clearer, as if the blinders had been removed from her eyes. Hope sprang up within her.

Before going back inside, she took one last deep breath and, when she exhaled, she felt revitalized, yet calm. Lighter. It was as if a weight had been lifted off her. The heaviness in her chest was gone. Tessa didn't want to analyze what had happened. She was just thankful her mind and heart were finally at peace.

She knew what she had to do.

First things first. Tessa picked up the phone and dialed a familiar number. "Hey, got a minute? I need your help."

‹›❧‹›

Getting ready to leave, Tessa took one last look in the full-length mirror that hung on the bathroom wall. It was a big day and she was a little nervous. Examining herself from every angle, she was pleased with her reflection. Then something caught her eye, actually, it was the *absence* of something. Earrings. She went to her dresser in search of just the right ones.

After opening a couple of compartments in the white jewelry case, she remembered that the specific pair she was looking for was in the antique box in the top drawer. She retrieved the handmade, oak heirloom.

When she opened the lid, her breath caught. Dylan's ring. She'd forgotten she'd put it in there with her other jewelry for safekeeping after he left. She picked it up and slipped it on her index finger. On her small hand, it flipped and spun around like a carnival ride.

Tessa smiled, though her eyes were cloudy with unshed tears. Running her fingers over the raised edges and engravings, she thought about the man who left it there.

"I'll have to get this back to him," she whispered softly.

The clock on her desk chimed and drew her back to her original task. She found the earrings she was looking for, put them on, then grabbed her purse and keys before rushing out the door. She couldn't be late.

Not today.

CHAPTER 23

Dylan's clothes were still a little stiff. The military had issued new cammies to him at the base in Germany when they discharged him, since the clothes he'd arrived in had been bloody and torn. At least he was able to keep his boots. Dylan was thankful he didn't have to break in new ones.

"You look deep in thought, sir," commented a baby-faced Marine who was sitting next to Dylan on the bus transporting them from the plane to the welcome home gathering across the base. "Got someone special waitin' for you?" He didn't pause for an answer. "Oh, man, I can't wait to see my girl! We're gonna get married in a couple of months."

Dylan forced a half grin and shook the young man's

hand. "Congratulations, Corporal." Leaning back against the seat, Dylan closed his eyes, hoping to ward off any further conversation.

Besides, he didn't have an answer to the question he'd been asked. All he could do now was wait.

And that was something Dylan didn't like doing.

ᏒᏂᏒᏂ

Tessa paced the floor while staring at her watch every few seconds. In a way, it seemed like just the other day, and yet so long ago, since she'd been here. The same small room, the same gray paint—the same secret window. Dylan was coming home today, and she needed to see for herself that he was okay.

"Where is that stupid bus? It was supposed to be here an hour ago," she mumbled. Another fifteen minutes passed then a faint, but familiar, click sounded behind her.

"They'll be here in ten." Mike's voice was soft but clear.

Inhaling and exhaling a long overdue sigh, she responded without turning around. "Thanks. For everything."

"You're sure this is how you want to do this?"

"Yes. It's the only way."

The minutes ticked by even slower than before. Her emotions were a jumbled mess. Her palms were sweating, and the flutters in her stomach were so intense she felt as if tiny gymnasts were in there practicing for the Olympics. Vans representing the local TV stations had arrived, the military band had just finished setting up, and families were putting the finishing touches on banners they secured to the fence outside. Rapid movements and loud noises on the other side of the window drew her attention. The bus was here. Her heart hammered in her chest, and her throat felt as dry as the Arizona desert in the middle of summer.

The Marines filed out of the bus and walked toward their waiting loved ones. As always, there were the unfortunate few who had nobody there to greet them, and they hurried through the groups of people and out of sight. Tessa's heart broke for those men and women.

Then she spotted him. The sight of him stole her breath for a second. Tessa watched him exit the bus and walk down the steps, chin up, and shoulders back. As he made his way through the groups of crying and happy spouses, parents, and children, she saw him look around cautiously, searching the crowd.

Dylan wondered if Tessa would show up, but it was glaringly apparent she'd decided not to. His heart sank at the thought that what they'd shared meant so little to her, that his love wasn't enough. But a part of him wasn't all that surprised.

Tessa watched his expression change. Sadness, like a shadow, fell across his face when he didn't find her there waiting for him. So focused on Dylan, she did not hear the sound of the door behind her.

"It's time."

"Are you sure? Can't I have just one more minute, please?"

"I'm afraid not, Tessa. You have to go now or it will be too late."

Such an eerily similar conversation transpired between them a few months ago. "All right," she conceded.

Mike led her back down the same gray hallway as before. But this time, when they came to the end, he motioned to the left, instead of toward the exit on her right that she'd used on her last visit.

He smiled and hugged her tight. "Go get him, girl!"

When he turned to leave, she caught a glimpse of his wet eyelashes. "You're crying," she cooed.

"Shush! No, I'm not." He looked around to make sure nobody had heard her. "It's probably my allergies to the dust or...asbestos, or who knows what's in this old building?"

Tessa chuckled and gave him a quick peck on the cheek. "You're such a big softy," she whispered in his ear.

He grinned. "Don't spread it around."

Her red, high heels clicked on the concrete as she made her way to the door that led to Dylan. Straightening her dress, she took a deep breath to calm her nerves. Would he forgive her? Would he give her a second chance? Or had she waited too long, hurt him too badly? She closed her eyes and sent up a silent prayer.

Rounding the corner of the building, Tessa walked toward the man that had been consuming her thoughts and dreams for the last few months. Despite the fact that Dylan had been traveling for several hours, all Tessa could think about was how wonderful he looked to her at that very moment.

He was thinner than the last time she'd seen him, but that didn't matter. He was still very handsome in his cammies.

Dylan stopped short when he saw her. *She did come.* He didn't want to appear too eager to see her until he knew what she had to say. Tessa had never given him an answer in the letter she sent while he was in the hospital. His insides trembled with excitement and uneasiness. He'd just come back from the war, and facing her here and now made him more nervous than any Taliban army. "I—I didn't know if you'd show or not."

Tessa stared into his rugged face. She'd rehearsed what she wanted to say to him over the last two days. But now that he was in front of her, she had a difficult time getting her mouth to work.

"I almost didn't."

Hearing her say those words was like a punch in the gut. "Then why did you?"

"I just couldn't stay away." She paused. "How are you?"

He shrugged then set his backpack down to the ground without breaking eye contact with her.

She attempted a smile. "You look good."

He let his gaze sweep over her quickly, but put on his best poker face. He wouldn't tip his hand just yet. "You, too."

Shifting her weight from one foot to the other, she fidgeted with her thumbnail before continuing with their conversation. "Umm—"

"Look, Tessa. I don't feel like dancing around each other right now with meaningless small talk."

She hung her head, knowing he was right. But what could she say? Before she responded, she stared up into his dark brown eyes. "I know I've made a mess of things."

There was no confirmation or denial of her statement on his face.

"I'm sorry, Dylan."

"I'm not looking for an apology from you, Tessa. I want more than that, and if you can't see a future for us, there's really nothing more to say." He leaned over and reached for his pack.

Tessa took a step closer to him. "Wait."

When he met her gaze, his eyes were hard and challenging.

"For what? So you can give me your list of excuses." *How could she do this? Show up here looking so beautiful and smelling so good.* It was that same perfume he carried with him. It sent his senses reeling with desire. *And now she was going to walk away—again?* His jaw clenched. "No, thanks. If that's why you're here, you shouldn't have bothered to get all dressed up. I need to go. Goodbye, Tessa."

He reached for his bag again, but before he could lift it off the pavement, he felt her hand on his arm.

Even though the words were harsh, they were true, and they cut straight through her. The fighter in her took over. She'd come too far, been though too much. She wasn't going to lose him. Not now. "Hold on one second, Mr. Cooper. I'm not done talking to you yet."

He straightened and arched his eyebrows, "Excuse me?"

"I'm not here to give you any excuses. Actually—" She paused and lifted her chin. "I'm here to tell you that I've changed my mind."

"Oh?"

"I tried to ignore and rationalize away how I felt, but I couldn't. So I'm here to ask if you would please consider giving me another chance."

Her voice shook slightly, but her eyes held the determination of the woman he had met long ago. At first, he was thrilled, but skepticism skittered up his spine. "Those are nice words, Tessa, but I'm not convinced. How do I know you won't turn and run the next time you get scared or think you've made a mistake? This isn't a game. It's for the long haul."

"I understand, and you need to know there are going to be times when I *will* get scared, but I want to build my future with you. I love you, Dylan."

At first, he was shocked, thinking he'd misunderstood her. When he realized what Tessa had said, he felt elated. Finally, the words he'd prayed to hear. But as quickly as his hopes had risen, they were crushed, when a ray of sun sparkled off a familiar piece of gold jewelry. "How can you say you're ready to be with me when you're still wearing *that*?" he said, nodding toward the chain around her neck.

A playful smile curved her lips as she planted her hands on her hips. "Lift it and see for yourself," she dared him.

Dylan hesitated for a moment, not sure if she was toying with his emotions or not. Tentatively, he slid his fingers under the tiny gold links, brushing them against the silky skin on her neck. In spite of the fact that she'd told him to, he felt her inhale sharply at his touch. He lifted the chain from under the neckline of her dress and, suddenly, his eyes opened wide. There, dangling at the end—his Marine Corps ring.

"Is that mine?" Dylan let the gold chain slip through his fingers until the ring he'd left behind for her to remember him by lay in the palm of his hand.

"Yes." Her voice was hushed as she covered his hand with hers.

"Where's Ben's ring?"

"At home, put away with his other memories."

"I'm not trying to erase him—"

"I appreciate that, but it's time. He's my past and you're my future. I finally know what I want. I've found the perfect man for me."

"Is that so?"

"Yup." Tessa reached up and gently touched the top of his head. "He stands about this tall. He's very good-looking and strong and brave. But he can be so, so sweet."

Dylan looked confused.

She lowered her hand to rest on his shoulder before continuing. "The perfect man for me is a gunny who is very sexy in his Marine Corps dress blues." Tessa started to giggle as a tear slipped down her cheek. "I love you, Sergeant Dylan Cooper, with all my heart."

He pulled her into his arms and she cried while he held her in his strong embrace.

He was so happy, he thought his heart would burst with love for her. They shared a quick, but passionate kiss. "Are you sure you're willing to take a chance and risk your heart again?"

"Absolutely." She gazed up at him as tears of pure joy filled her eyes. "It appears I'm destined to love a Marine. But maybe you could put in for a less stressful assignment—like becoming a drill instructor."

They both laughed. Dylan picked her up and twirled her around. "By the way, you look absolutely gorgeous," he growled seductively in her ear. "I can't wait to get you alone and show you how much I've missed you."

Tessa squealed with delight as her arms encircled his neck. "Sounds good to me."

Other guys around them whooped, hollered, and clapped. After setting her down, he took a step back. He realized there was something he needed to do. Reaching up, he tenderly held her face. "I know this isn't the most romantic place—" He chuckled. "—and I don't have a diamond ring, but I love you so much, Tessa. Will you marry me?"

"Yes. Yes, of course I will."

"Even if I stay in the Marine Corps until I retire?"

With love overflowing from her eyes, Tessa nodded. "Semper Fi, Sergeant Cooper. Forever."

About the Author

Debbie Lee was born and raised in South Dakota but currently lives in Arizona. She raised 2 daughters, Nicole and Katie, and she is extremely proud of the wonderful women they have become. She has worked for the State of Arizona as an Administrative Assistant for the last 25 years. Lee started writing in 2009 and enjoys reading contemporary romances mixed with a little humor. She's thankful to God for all the blessings in her life and for this new adventure as a writer. Lee is a huge animal lover, and especially enjoys spending time with her four-legged Chihuahua "grandchildren," Bruiser and Dottie.